WHEN THE CLOCK

STRIKES THIRTEEN

Lois Cloarec Hart
L.T. Smith
Emma Weimann
Joan Arling
Diane Marina
Erzabet Bishop
R.G. Emanuelle

Ylva

CONTENTS

Introduction   1

Midnight Messages by Lois Cloarec Hart   3

Batteries Not Included by L.T. Smith   27

Lost and Found by Emma Weimann   49

Chrysalis by Joan Arling   83

Sisters of the Moon by Diane Marina   93

Wolf Moon by Erzabet Bishop   125

Love Bites by R.G. Emanuelle   149

About the Authors   177

Other books from Ylva Publishing

Coming from Ylva Publishing in 2014

INTRODUCTION

Fantasy is one of my favorite genres—if not my most favorite one. I love the thrill of the unknown, of the things and beings that (could) exist without most of us acknowledging their existence. When I went to Ireland a few years ago, I dreamed of meeting a faerie—and maybe I did without even knowing. In England, I feared and hoped to stumble across a White Lady, and in Edinburgh, I would have given everything to hear the drummer ghost of Edinburgh Castle.

Unfortunately, I didn't. But I haven't given up hope for the future.

Until then, I continue to dream and publish stories that portray a reality different from the one we experience every day.

For this anthology, I had a range of wonderful authors contributing their stories as well as a talented graphic artist and a meticulous editor.

You'll find a variety of the otherworldly and supernatural that will keep you glued to your seat.

Enjoy the read and never stop dreaming…

Astrid Ohletz
Publisher

MIDNIGHT MESSAGES
by Lois Cloarec Hart

LUCE SHEPPARD TOWELLED her hair dry, averting her eyes from the large bathroom mirror. It was habit, born seven years ago and now so deeply ingrained that she never considered the implications.

This time, however, as she slid the towel over her chest, Luce stopped. With a deep breath, she lowered the towel and looked at her reflection. Her gaze fell on the scar, then slid to the right and focused on the barest shadow, the slightest indication that the curve of her breast was not as it should be. Luce wasn't even sure whether it was just her imagination.

For seven years Luce had been scrupulous about her monthly self-examination. Yet she hadn't noticed the anomaly until ten days ago when she woke with her fingertips resting against that very spot.

Ten days, and every waking hour since, she had thought of little else. But tonight Luce had finally come to a decision, one that she could live with.

"Or not." Luce tossed her towel aside and drew a brush through her short, silver hair. When her curls had been temporarily disciplined into a smooth cap, she dropped the brush on the counter and padded into the bedroom.

Luce smiled at the small, white Shih-tzu-bichon mix curled up and snoozing on her side of the bed. The elderly dog didn't stir as Luce opened the window. She shivered at the rush of cool night air and quickly slipped beneath the covers. "Ferron, move over, you bed hog."

The dog grudgingly rearranged herself and settled back down.

Rain pounded outside. She loved the sound. It reminded

her of camping, snuggled next to Beth in a sleeping bag, listening to the rain patter on the tent. But that was long ago. Carefree trips were long ago. Beth was long ago.

With a sigh, Luce turned on her side and closed her eyes. Ferron butted up against her back and emitted a yawn. For the first time in ten nights, Luce allowed the comforting warmth of her companion and the sound of the rain to carry her into a peaceful sleep.

∾

Luce startled awake at an unfamiliar sound. She opened her eyes and glanced at the bedside clock. *4:44.* "Aw, crap, don't tell me they're partying across the street again."

Luce hurled mental lightning bolts at her young neighbour who was notorious for his all-night revelry. She had lost count of the number of times his inconsideration had kept her awake or woken her early as his guests stumbled on their way in the wee hours. "Should've known I wouldn't get through a Saturday night without those idiots making enough noise to wake the dead."

Luce made a determined effort to return to sleep. But just as she was drifting off, the sound rose in volume again.

Goddamn it! Luce thumped her pillow in frustration and then realization set in. It wasn't, as she'd first thought, some inebriated woman laughing as she departed the neighbour's house. Someone was crying.

Startled, Luce bolted up and dislodged Ferron.

"Are you all right?" Her call out the open window went unanswered. She cocked her head to listen, unsure of what she should do next.

The weeping seemed more distant, as if the crier had moved further down the sidewalk.

It was definitely a young woman in distress. *What if she's been assaulted?* Living in a good neighbourhood was no guarantee of safety, so Luce scrambled out of bed. After throwing on a pair of jeans, a T-shirt, and an ancient cardigan, she hurried to the front door, followed by a confused dog.

"No, Ferron, stay here." Luce opened the door. The street seemed empty and quiet, and for a moment she doubted her own senses. She wrapped the sweater tightly around herself and went down the long flight of steps, grateful that the night's heavy rain had subsided to mere mist. When she reached the sidewalk, Luce looked north and south, and then saw her.

A teenager clutching an oversized handbag stood on the sidewalk, three or four houses down. She stared out into the street, still weeping, but in an exhausted monotone, as if she had run out of energy for anything more.

"Are you all right?" Luce tried again. "Are you lost?"

"Lost?"

"Yes. Are you lost?"

"I'm not lost...exactly. I just don't know where to go."

Well, that's one definition of lost. There was something so despondent in the girl's body language that Luce made an instant decision. "Look, why don't you come inside and get warm? We'll figure something out."

As the girl drew nearer, Luce saw that she was drenched, her hair matted and her bedraggled jeans soaked. "Good heavens, how long have you been out in this storm?"

"I don't know. All night, I guess."

Luce pushed aside the questions that sprang to mind and led the way back to her house and up the stairs. "Not to worry. We'll get you dry and warm, and figure out how to get you home."

Ferron barked sharply as they reached the door and the girl flinched.

"Oh, don't worry about her. She's completely harmless, all sound and fury as it were. Come on in." Luce shooed Ferron away and gestured to the couch. "Why don't you take a seat?"

The girl looked down at herself. "I don't want to get it wet."

"Just a moment." Luce found an old towel in the linen closet and returned to the living room.

The girl still stood in the entryway.

Luce stretched the towel over the back and seat cushion of the couch. "There you go. Make yourself comfortable."

The girl kicked off her shoes and set her bag on the mat. Luce retreated to her chair. The girl settled on the towel and glanced around.

"My name is Luce Sheppard. What's yours?"

"Keira. Keira Keller."

Luce regarded her slender, dark-haired visitor. She estimated the girl to be about sixteen or seventeen. Whatever had traumatized Keira had certainly left its imprint on her features. Though there were no visible marks on her person, Keira's swollen eyes held a bleak expression. Luce briefly wondered if Keira was sober, but there had been no intoxication evident in her speech. "Well, Keira, you're obviously in trouble. I'd like to help if I'm able. Can you tell me what happened tonight?"

Keira blinked twice and her eyes began to well with tears.

Luce hastily passed a box of tissue. "Whatever happened, you're safe now. I'm not going to turn you out onto the streets. I really do want to help, so take your time. Maybe you'd like a cup of something warm. Tea? Coffee? Some hot chocolate?"

Ferron sniffed around Keira's feet, but this time the girl didn't recoil. She blew her nose loudly and dropped her hand to pet the dog. Ferron took that as an invitation and jumped up on the couch.

"Ferron, get down."

Keira shook her head. "No, it's okay." She pulled the edge of the large towel over her clothes and gathered Ferron onto her lap.

Luce smiled. It was just like Ferron to worm her way onto a willing lap. "About that something warm?"

"No, thank you, Ms Sheppard."

"Luce, please. So, how did you come to be wandering my street?"

"I told my mom I was going to stay at my best friend's house, and Shelley told her parents that we were going to stay at my place." Keira shot Luce a shamefaced look.

"Let me guess—you were actually planning to go to a party." *Though not across the street, apparently.*

Keira ducked her head. "Eddie's parents are out of town, so most of the school was going to be at his place. Shelley said Tyler was going to be there and he really wanted me to come, but it was all lies."

"Tyler wasn't there?"

"Oh, he was there all right. He just couldn't have cared less that *I* was there. He and Shelley had planned it so that they could have a whole night together. She needed me to give her an alibi, and since she knew I was interested in Tyler, she used that to convince me to lie to Mom. I never lie to my mom."

"Did you know they were...um, seeing each other?"

Keira frowned indignantly. "Of course not. I wouldn't have been such an idiot if Shelley had told me she and Tyler were hooking up. Now I'm not even going to be able to go back to school. It's too humiliating!"

"I'm sure it's not nearly as bad as you think."

"It is, believe me. When I opened the bathroom door and saw them together, I screamed. Everyone came running. I felt like such a fool. Tyler was cursing, Shelley yelled at me to grow up. And you just know someone's already put it on Facebook." Keira heaved a deep sigh. "I am so going to be the butt of all the jokes at school on Monday. It's probably gone viral by now."

Luce sent a brief thanks heavenward that she'd grown up when the fastest way to communicate with the greatest number of people was to write on a bathroom wall. *Or tell Jessie.* She smiled at the thought of her oldest and dearest friend. "Okay, I see how this all happened, but why didn't you call your mom for a ride home?"

"I couldn't do that. If I called Mom, then she'd know we weren't at Shelley's place, and she'd tell Mr. and Mrs. Blythe."

"Uh-huh. So even after what Shelley did, you didn't want to blow the whistle on her deceit?"

Keira regarded Luce as if she had grown a second head. "And get a rep as a rat? Are you crazy? Besides, Shelley's still my best friend. We never stay mad at each other for long. Anyway, I ran out of the house so fast that I had no time to call. I didn't have any idea where to go so I've just been walking the streets for hours and hours. I don't even know where I am."

"You're on Wood Springs Crescent. But surely you have a cell. It's been years since I've seen anyone your age without one of those electronic leashes."

"Well, yeah, but I sort of…" Keira's voice trailed off to an inaudible murmur.

Luce leaned forward. "I'm sorry, you did what?"

"I was so shocked when Tyler yelled at me that I threw my phone at him. It hit the shower tiles and broke into a hundred pieces."

Luce tried to stifle her mirth, but failed. Ferron lifted her head at her mistress's laughter and Keira stared indignantly.

But just as Luce began to regain control and dabbed at her wet eyes, Keira chuckled. "I guess it was pretty dumb, but you know what was even dumber?"

Luce shook her head. "No idea."

"Them. All they had to do was lock the bathroom door. How much common sense does that take, for crying out loud?"

That set Luce off again, and this time Keira joined in.

When the laughter subsided, Luce felt better than she had in many days. "Okay, here's what we're going to do—I'll loan you a set of sweats so you can dry off, and you're welcome to stay here for what's left of the night. In the morning I'll give you a ride home. How does that sound?"

"Not that I don't appreciate it, but my mom is still going to ground me for a year."

"Do you want to call and let her know where you are?"

Keira glanced at the phone on the side table next to her. "No, thanks. I don't want to wake her yet. Hey, Luce?"

"Yes?"

"Did you know you've got seventeen unanswered messages on your machine?"

"Yes, I know." *Jessie is nothing if not persistent.*

"An ex-husband you're avoiding?"

"No, just my best friend trying to set me up on a date that I'm not interested in. She's not good at taking no for an answer, so sometimes I find it easier to simply not answer the phone."

"Huh. Hey, Luce?"

"Yes, Keira?"

"You mentioned hot chocolate?"

"I did. Would you like some?"

"Please and thank you."

"All right. There's a guest room and bath down the hall to the left. There are clean towels hung, and some old sweats in the bureau. Help yourself, and come back out when you're ready. I'll have the hot chocolate waiting."

Keira carefully dislodged Ferron from her lap and set the small dog on the floor. Luce smiled. The young woman might be a typical teen, riddled with the usual adolescent angst, but she clearly had a gentle, considerate heart.

When Keira returned fifteen minutes later, Luce chuckled. Though now clean, and mostly dry, Keira looked like a child playing dress-up. She had rolled up the pant legs and sleeves several times over, but when she accepted the proffered hot chocolate, her hand was almost lost in fabric.

Keira put the drink down and folded up the damp towel she'd been sitting on. Setting it aside, she took her seat as Ferron jumped up into her lap.

Luce sipped her hot chocolate as she watched her visitor cautiously raise the steaming cup to her lips. Keira appeared to be much calmer, and was definitely more cheerful. "Are you feeling better?"

Keira tilted her head as she considered Luce's question. "I think so. You know what really hurts, though?"

Luce could think of several possibilities, but she shook her head.

"It's not just that Shelley lied to me when she knows me well enough to know she didn't need to. It was the way she used me. We've been best friends since second grade. How could she do that to me? Over a stupid boy."

"I don't think I'm the best person to answer that. But here's a thought: Maybe Tyler was potentially interested in you. Maybe she needed to ensure he'd only pay attention to her, so she made sure the bathroom door wasn't locked. Even if it hadn't been you who opened the door, Shelley was flaunting her connection with Tyler the moment someone opened the door and saw what was going on."

Keira snorted. "Well, she certainly was flaunting everything she had the way she was dressed tonight, and believe me, she has lots to flaunt. Not like me," she added glumly, glancing at her less than ample chest cloaked in the shapeless sweatshirt.

The girl's innocent words landed like a battering ram. Luce carefully set her cup aside, unable to enjoy the rich flavour as she fought to retain her hard-won equanimity.

"Did I say something wrong?" Keira regarded Luce with a worried expression. "You've got this really weird look on your face."

"No, no, not at all. It's probably just a bit of indigestion. I'm no longer at an age when I can eat or drink at all hours and not pay the consequences."

Aware that Keira's keen eyes were fixed on her, Luce forced a smile, but knew her attempt was less than convincing.

Keira nodded at the blinking answering machine. "Why don't you want to answer those calls?"

"I told you. My best friend has been trying to fix me up on a date, and I'm not interested."

"Why aren't you interested? Is he, like, a jerk?"

"I have no idea, and you have the pronoun wrong."

"Pardon?"

"My friend tells me she knows a really nice woman she's sure would be perfect for me." Luce waited for Keira's reaction.

Keira shrugged. "Okay, so what's wrong? If your best friend is recommending her, why not say 'yes'? You don't know if this person might be 'the one'. You'll *never* know if you don't at least have the first date."

"As has been vividly demonstrated for you tonight, sometimes best friends make very bad choices."

"Shelley was an idiot, but she's 16. We're supposed to be idiots at 16. What's your excuse?"

"Excuse me? I don't think I need one. I just prefer my current state of singleness."

"No, you don't. Some people do, and that's cool, but you're not one of them."

Luce blinked. *What the...?*

"Are you chickening out because of a bad break-up?"

"I, uh, well, there was a woman..."

"What happened?"

Keira's question uncorked the bottle. "After twelve years together, Beth left me for someone else, just when I needed her the most. When I was fighting with everything in me to preserve our future together, she just...left. I came home from the hospital to find a house echoing with empty. She was gone, and so were all our belongings. The only thing she left behind were my clothes, books thrown on the floor, and a litre of sour milk in the fridge. She even took the light bulbs out of their sockets, for God's sake. Not to mention that she cleaned out our joint bank accounts. Her timing was perfect. Beth knew damned well I wouldn't have the energy to fight her, so she got away with lock, stock, and barrel. I had to start again from scratch, when I barely had the energy to make it from my borrowed air mattress to the bathroom. It's a good thing my best friend was caring for Ferron, or Beth probably would've dumped her at the shelter, just like she dumped me."

Keira didn't flinch from the bitterness in Luce's words. "So, Beth was a total bitch. That doesn't mean Jessie's friend is, and there's no way you can know unless you say 'yes'. So what's the real reason you don't want this date?"

"It wouldn't be fair."

"To who? You, or Jessie's friend?"

"Either, I guess."

"Why not?"

"You are just full of questions, aren't you?"

"My mom says I started asking questions at eighteen months and haven't stopped yet. But I also know when someone is dodging a question."

"Hey, don't you want to get some sleep? You're going to be exhausted come morning."

"I'm a teenager. By definition, I'm a night owl. And you're still avoiding the question."

"Well, I'm *not* a teenager, and I'm going to bed." Luce began to rise from her chair, determined to get what little sleep she could before it was time to deliver this aggravating, impudent child back to her mother.

"Avoidance."

The word was quiet, but something about the way Keira said it stopped Luce in her tracks. She sank back into her chair.

"Why won't you let Jessie set you up?"

"Because I'm going to die."

Later—much later—Luce would remember the curious absence of shock on her visitor's youthful face.

"You don't know that for sure."

"Yes, Keira, I do. I'm not going to fight the cancer this time. I fought like the Hounds of Hades were after me last time, and I literally went through hell. I'm not going to do it again. I...can't do it again. Since Beth...well, there's no compelling reason for me to fight."

"So you're just going to give up?"

A flash of anger coursed through Luce at the girl's casual assertion. "Give up? I like to think that I'm accepting the inevitable as gracefully as I can. You know how you always see in the Obituaries that so-and-so waged a long and courageous battle against one disease or another? Well, they can write that I'm a coward, if they want, but I'm leaving the ring. To continue the metaphor, I'm not even going to answer the bell this time. And there's absolutely nothing they can say to change my mind."

"Who are 'they'?"

"Excuse me?"

"You said 'they'. As in 'they' can write whatever 'they' want, and 'they' can't change your mind. So, who are 'they'?"

"Well, I guess…Jessie, and my other friends."

"None of whom would want you to fight?"

Luce considered Keira's point. "I love them very much, and I know they love me…"

"But?"

Luce settled deeper in her chair. It had all seemed so simple when she'd finalized her decision mere hours earlier. "I should be able to 'go gentle into that good night' if I want to. Why isn't it okay to accept the inevitable? Why do I have to fight? Why does our culture esteem those who by doing so make their lives living hells, and disdain those who know all life is finite and choose to live whatever time they have left on their own terms?"

"Because those who fight aren't just fighting for themselves, they're fighting for the ones they love—fighting to stay with them a little longer. Isn't it the most natural thing in the world to wish your loved ones could stay with you for as long as possible? Surely Jessie and your friends would grieve your loss."

"Of course, but they've all got families to comfort and support them. It may take time, but they'll be fine. The bottom line is that it's my choice."

"Agreed, and if you're making that choice out of conviction, guided solely by a desire for a peaceful and productive conclusion to your life, then cool. But if you're doing it because you're unwilling to fight for another chance to share your heart, share your life, then it's cowardice. That's all I'm saying."

Luce stared at Keira. "What are you—a sixty-year-old in a sixteen-year-old body?"

Keira laughed and shook her head. "I guess I'm just channelling my grandmother. She's about the smartest woman I know."

"I'm sure she'd be gratified to hear that."

"I've told her. Me and Granddame are tight. Mom's a single

mother, has been since my father walked out two months after I was born, so Granddame helped raise me."

"They've done an excellent job."

Keira grinned. "Thanks. I'll have to tell Granddame."

"But not your mom?"

Keira shook her head. "Mom can't seem to hear me when I talk, and she's going to be pissed when she learns I lied to her. That's always been her one absolute rule—no lies between us."

"I'm sure that knowing you're safe will be all that matters to your mother."

A wistful expression crossed the girl's face. "Maybe. Me and Granddame love Mom like crazy, but sometimes I think she gets so caught up in her work and all that she forgets that. I'll get my grandmother to talk to her. Granddame is better than me at handling Mom, though I know she'll insist I give it a try. She always does."

Ferron chose that moment to yawn and stretch.

Luce chuckled and yawned in response. "I believe her Ladyship has the right idea. I think we should all retire for a couple of hours. Is your mom expecting you home at a certain time? Should I set the alarm?"

"No, that's okay. Mom knows Shelley and I usually sleep until noon when we're together."

"All right then, we'll sleep until we're ready to rise, and then get you home." Luce rose, undeterred this time. "If you need anything, just holler. I'm a very light sleeper."

"Okay, thanks. Hey, Luce, I really appreciate this. It's not everyone who would open their door to a stranger."

"I wouldn't open my door to just any stranger, but you looked like you could use some help. I'm glad I heard you crying." Luce shuddered as she thought of some of the places Keira could've ended up.

"I am too. I wish…"

"You wish…?"

"It doesn't matter now. Sleep well, Luce. I enjoyed our talk."

"Goodnight, Keira." Luce smiled as Keira walked down the

hall to the guest room. *I did too. Who knew a kid could debate like that? I'd love to meet her grandmother...or maybe not. Granddame sounds like she could talk a bear out of a honey factory. I'm not so sure I want that right now.*

Bemused, Luce opened the door for Ferron and ignored the indignant look she got in response. "Oh, go on. It's not even raining anymore, for heaven's sake."

Grumbling, Ferron went outside and scooted back in moments later.

Luce looked around. The street was still quiet. None of her neighbours would have the slightest clue that anything untoward had occurred during the night, but Luce knew it would be a long time before she forgot the unexpectedly thought-provoking questions of her midnight visitor.

✧

"So when I got up, just before nine, Keira was already gone. She left my sweats folded on the bed, which, by the way, didn't even look like it had been slept in. And she left a note that she'd contacted her grandmother, who was coming to pick her up. So, all's well that ends well." Luce sat back in satisfaction at a tale well told.

Jessie blinked at her. "All's well that ends well? Are you out of your pea-picking mind? She could've been a psychopath, and you just took her in off the street. She could've murdered you in your sleep!"

"Well, she didn't. Look, she was just a good kid who had a lapse in judgment. I couldn't leave her outside. God knows what could've happened. You know bloody well that *you* wouldn't have ignored her either."

"Like hell."

Luce shook her head sceptically. She'd seen Jessie's big heart in action too many times to believe the denial.

The waitress approached, but Jessie waved her off. "No more for me, thanks. Luce?"

"No, I'm good. Just the check, please."

Jessie returned to the topic that had consumed much of their Sunday brunch. "So, you got her full name, right? Are you going to Google her or check her Facebook page or anything?"

"Why would I?"

"I don't know—to see if she was telling the truth?"

"Again, why? It's not like she had anything to gain by being less than completely honest with me, so why wouldn't I take her at her word? It certainly doesn't change my life one way or the other." Even as Luce spoke the words, she knew they were untrue. It was less than five hours since she'd bade Keira goodnight, and she'd been unable to get the girl's argument out of her mind.

Luce regarded her friend. Jessie had been there for her unstintingly before and after Beth's betrayal. She had deputized her extended family and they'd all seen Luce through the enervating medical procedures, driven her to appointments, cooked meals, cleaned the house, and cared for Ferron. Jessie then nursed Luce through the aftermath of surgery and a broken heart. What would Jessie say if she knew that the cancer had returned and Luce had all but decided not to suffer through the extreme measures that might beat it this time?

Luce knew without asking that Jessie would be there again, if needed. Luce also knew she had to make a final decision soon. In the meantime however, there was one small thing she could do to make Jessie's day, a small repayment for all Jessie had done for her. "About your friend, the one you keep trying to set me up on a date with…"

"You'll do it? You'll give Stephanie a chance? I swear you won't regret it. Plus, Ms Goody Two Shoes, you'll be doing a good deed, as well."

"How so?"

"Stephanie's had a really tough year, and despite my best efforts she's turned into something of a hermit. Truthfully, I'm not even sure I can persuade her into going on a date with you, but I just know you two are perfect for each other."

"For crying out loud, Jessie. You don't even know if the woman wants to go out with me and you've been badgering me non-stop for three weeks? What the hell were you thinking?"

"I was thinking that two women I care very much about needed each other."

Jessie's simple answer defused Luce's pique. "Jesus. All right, if you can set it up, let me know where to be and when. You know my schedule as well as I do."

Jessie jumped to her feet and darted around the table to hug Luce. "Excellent! You won't regret this, I swear."

Luce patted Jessie's arms and winced at the strength of her hug. "All right, already."

Jessie released Luce and glanced at her watch. "Oops, I've got to get going. Roy has old timer's hockey this afternoon and I promised I'd be home to take over the kids by one."

"Give Lucy a hug for me, and tell Brian I'll be by after work tomorrow to give him a hand."

"You really are the best. God knows Roy and I are at a loss when it comes to computer meltdowns, so I really appreciate Auntie Luce riding to the rescue."

"My pleasure. But don't forget I was promised homemade chocolate chip cookies in payment."

"Brian's already bribed his sister to make a batch for you. I'll give you a call later, after I talk to Stephanie."

Luce wondered what kind of pressure Jessie had exerted on Stephanie to convince the reclusive woman to meet so swiftly. It had only been noon when Luce had finally agreed, and here she was a few hours later waiting in a restaurant for her blind date. She eyed the woman who had just entered and was talking to the hostess. The stranger was about Luce's age, with dark hair and a weary look on her face. Her clothes hung loosely, as if she'd recently lost a great deal of weight.

The hostess led the woman to Luce's table and Luce stood to greet her date. She extended her hand. "Hi, I'm Luce Sheppard."

The woman shook Luce's hand. "I'm Stephanie Carroll. It's nice to meet you."

As Stephanie bent to take a seat, a chain dangling from her neck got caught on the clasp of her purse and broke. A large gold locket bounced across the table, popping open as it struck the edge. The woman cried out in dismay as Luce made a hasty grab and saved the locket from falling to the floor.

"No harm done. I'm sure you can have the chain repaired, and the locket…" Luce scanned the exterior, "the locket looks fine." Then she stared at the photo. "Hey, I recognize her."

"I'm sure you do." Stephanie's voice was cool as she put out her hand for the locket. "The damned news media were most intrusive at the time."

Intrigued by the coincidence, Luce didn't process her dinner companion's words. "It's Keira." She looked up with a grin. "Are you Keira's mom? Hey, you have the coolest kid. I really enjoyed talking to her last night. I hope you weren't too hard on her when she got home."

Stephanie's face went white. "Is this your idea of a joke? What kind of sadist are you? Christ Almighty, do you strangle puppies and drown kittens, too? I hope you enjoyed your little laugh, now rot in hell!" She stood so abruptly that her chair toppled over. She snatched the locket out of Luce's hand and turned abruptly on her heel.

Stunned, Luce watched Stephanie rush from the restaurant.

A waiter discreetly righted the chair. "Will the lady be rejoining you, madam?"

Luce shook her head. "Somehow I doubt it. Uh, look, just bring me the check for the wine, and I'll call it a wrap." The waiter hurried off, while Luce went over and over her words. *What the hell did I say that upset her so? Crap! Maybe Keira hadn't talked to her yet. Damn, I hope I didn't get the kid in trouble.*

By the time Luce reached her house, Jessie was inside waiting for her. Without allowing Luce time to speak, Jessie lit into her. "What the hell were you thinking? What got into you to torture Stephanie like that? Do you know that right now she's crying her eyes out as if it just happened yesterday? Jesus Christ, Luce! I'd never have believed you capable of such insensitivity."

"Now just a goddamned minute, Jess. I haven't the faintest clue what you're talking about. All I know is that Keira's mom wigged out on me for no reason at all. Hell, I was complimenting her daughter and—"

"Whoa, whoa, whoa...what do you mean you were complimenting her daughter? Luce, Stephanie's daughter is dead. She died a year ago this weekend, that's why I thought it would be a good distraction for you two to go out. Get her mind off things for a bit."

"Dead? What are you talking about? I told you. I spent an hour talking to Keira last night, right here in my living room. Well, I guess it was more like really early this morning, but you know what I mean. Look, if I got it wrong, I'll apologize to her, but Stephanie's daughter sure looks a helluva lot like Keira. They could be twins."

Her face pale, Jessie stared at Luce. Without a word she turned and walked into the den where Luce's desktop was located.

Luce followed in confusion and watched as Jessie googled a name. Instantly a long list of hits attached to the name of Keira Marie Killian was provided. Jessie clicked on the top one. When a picture and article popped up, Jessie turned. "Is this the girl you invited off the street Saturday morning?"

Luce peered at the photo and nodded. "Yes, that's Keira." She began to read the article and instantly felt faint. She groped behind her for a chair and Jessie pushed one into her hand. "Oh, my God. Jess, is this true? You're not screwing with me?"

"You know me better than that. Would I ever joke about the death of a child?"

"No, of course not. How did I not know this? Something this sensationalistic had to be all over the media."

"Here, yes, but you were working in Saudi Arabia last fall."

Luce nodded. "And I had no time for anything but fulfilling our contract. No wonder I missed this."

"They found the killer within hours. Turned out to be a known sex offender who had left a bar and was walking home. They know his path crossed Keira's. No one's really sure what happened after that, but because he has a record a mile long and was in the police database as living in the neighbourhood where she disappeared, they found him before he even had time to dispose of the body. He pled guilty and they moved fast on sentencing. I think it must've been all over with a couple of weeks before you got back. I actually think that's part of Stephanie's current dilemma. It all happened so quickly that she really had no time to process everything. One day her daughter was alive and sneaking out to a party with her best friend, the next she was dead."

"I have to talk to Stephanie. I have to convince her I wasn't trying to...trying to... I just have to tell her I would never do what she thinks I did."

Jessie shook her head. "So you're going to try to convince her that you gave her daughter's ghost hot chocolate and a pair of your old sweats? There's no way she's going to listen to you now. I've known you for forty years and I'm having trouble believing you."

"But you know I wouldn't make it up. What possible reason would I have?" Luce stopped her protestation, as a thought struck her. "Hey, what about Keira's grandmother? The note said that her grandmother was coming to pick her up."

"I don't know about Stephanie's own mother, but her mother-in-law—the one who looked after Keira when Stephanie worked—died a couple months after Keira was murdered. Everyone said she died of a broken heart because the two of them were so tight. It doubled the blow, because Stephanie was very close to her mother-in-law. The three of them shared a home. Stephanie went back to her maiden name after the divorce, but she let Keira keep her father's last name as a tribute to her grandma."

"Granddame."

"Pardon?"

"Keira called her grandmother, Granddame. I thought it was really sweet."

"I never met the grandmother, I've only known Stephanie for a year. I initially met her through my work with Victims Services, and we got to be friends. Luce, you know I've had some tough cases, but in all my years with the Services, I don't think I've ever dealt with someone so completely shattered. The grandmother held Stephanie together for the first couple of months, then when she died, I thought for sure we were going to lose Stephanie too. She's only barely begun to live again in the last couple of months. Damn it, I hope this doesn't set her back. I'm not sure she'd survive going back to square one."

Luce reached for Jessie's hand. "You have to talk to Stephanie for me. You have to apologize on my behalf. I would never hurt another person that way, you know that."

"I do, but I don't know that Stephanie will listen. It took all my considerable powers of persuasion to talk her into meeting you for dinner. I don't think there's any possible future for you two, now."

"I don't expect there to be, but I feel terrible at having aggravated her grief. I just didn't know."

Jessie was quiet, spinning the office chair slowly left and right. "Do you think it really was Keira's ghost? I mean, that's pretty freaky, isn't it?"

"She sure seemed real to me and Ferron." *And she made her points like a Supreme Court Justice.*

"I have to get home. Look, I'll talk to Stephanie, but I make no promises."

"Thanks, Jess."

Thoroughly shaken, Luce walked Jessie to the back door and bade her goodbye. Then she knelt and looked under the kitchen table, where Ferron had hidden from the raised voices. "C'mon, you big chicken. Come out of there. Auntie Jess wasn't yelling at you."

Ferron emerged and trotted to her bowl, looking up expectantly.

"Hah, not a hope, munchkin. You had supper long before I went out, and don't try to tell me you didn't. You cannot be hungry." Luce rolled her eyes when her words had no effect on the waiting dog. "All right. One treat, and that's all you get." One treat turned into three as Luce picked Ferron up and went to her favourite chair.

Luce absently stroked Ferron while she rocked, as she tried to recall every moment of the odd encounter. "What do you think, old girl? Do you think we had a visitation? And if so, why? What's the message?"

Something flashed in her mind, and Luce stopped rocking. "Hey, I never told her Jessie's name...did I?" Her memory of Keira's visit was unusually vivid, and she was certain Keira had been the first to mention Jessie. "And how come I never heard her leave? You know the sound of a leaf falling normally wakes me up. Huh. *Normally*. But what's normal about this whole thing, eh, Ferron?"

Luce rocked some more, running her fingers through Ferron's coat as she reviewed the strange events of the weekend. Lost in her thoughts for almost an hour, Luce was startled when the doorbell rang. It set off a barking spree and Luce shushed Ferron as she set the dog down. She opened the front door and found Stephanie standing out on the stoop, half turned as if ready to dart away.

"Hey, hi. I'm really glad you came by so I can apologize in person." Luce pushed the door open and stepped aside. "Would you like to come in for coffee?"

After a long moment's hesitation, Stephanie stepped inside. Just as she had with Keira, Luce indicated the couch and gave her unexpected and obviously wary guest a wide berth as she went to the kitchen. When she returned, Luce found Stephanie sitting on the edge of the couch, cautiously petting Ferron who lay next to her feet.

Luce handed her a cup of coffee. "May I take your coat?"

Stephanie shook her head and pulled the loose coat more

tightly around her body.

Luce went to her rocking chair. "I take it Jessie called you?"

"Yes." Stephanie fixed desperate eyes on Luce. "Is it true? Please, I'm begging you to tell me the truth. Was Keira...here?"

"Let me ask you a question first. Does...did Keira call your mother-in-law 'Granddame'?"

Stephanie gasped. "Yes. How did you know? Did Jessie tell you?"

"No. When I brought it up, Jessie didn't know. Keira told me. And the answer to your first question is, yes, Keira was here. Let me tell you the whole story."

Luce related the events of early Sunday morning, careful not to omit anything, even the parts pertinent only to herself. She paused only to get some tissues for a weeping Stephanie. When she finished the story, her guest sat in silence for a few minutes.

Then Stephanie dried her eyes. "Did you by any chance..." she took a deep, shuddering breath, "keep her note?"

"Mmm, I threw it in the garbage, but it should still be there since I haven't taken the trash out yet. Just give me a moment." Luce picked through the trashcan and located the crumpled note under coffee grounds. It was badly stained, but the writing was still legible. She patted it dry and straightened it as best she could before she returned to the living room and handed it to Stephanie. "Sorry it's such a mess. If I'd known, I'd have taken better care of it."

"She was here." There was no doubt in Stephanie's voice as she stared at the note. "I'd know her handwriting anywhere, and here..." She pointed to a tiny Victorian-looking flourish under Keira's signature. "She always did this. She said it was to brand her signature and that someday, when she was famous, designers would clamour to use it." She shivered. "Who could've guessed she would become famous for such a hideous reason."

"I'm so sorry, Stephanie. Just from the brief time I spent with her, I know what a treasure you lost. My heart breaks for you, but I'm glad Keira came to me. Now you know she's not...well, completely gone, I guess."

"I've tried so hard to feel her presence, but all I can feel is the agony of losing her...of waking up each morning to my daughter's empty room, of never hearing her beautiful voice calling for me. Sometimes I think I'll go insane with the need to hold her. I even went to a medium who ended up giving me my money back. She said my grief was too strong for Keira to break through, and to come back when my grief had eased. As if it will ever ease."

"Keira did say that you weren't hearing her when she talks to you. I thought she meant the usual mother-teenage daughter communication problems. Maybe she meant that she's been trying to get through to you, but as the medium said, she can't reach you. So she had to find another way to go about it."

Stephanie looked up from the paper with a puzzled expression. "But why did she choose to come to you? We've never met before, have we?"

"No, but I expect Keira became aware of our mutual friend, Jessie, and decided to use that connection to make contact."

"Dear Jessie. She's been wonderful this past year. I must admit I was terribly harsh to her when she first began to bring up the possibility of me dating again. I actually haven't dated all that much since I came out in Keira's childhood, and I certainly wasn't interested, under the circumstances, but she has been unbelievably persistent."

Luce chuckled and pointed to the still blinking message machine. "Tell me about it. Persistence is Jess' middle name. Not to mention that I'm sure Keira and your mother-in-law were urging her on."

"Kate. Keira's grandmother's name was Kate. Losing her after losing Keira nearly had me looking for a way out myself."

"I'm glad you didn't, but what stopped you?"

"Two things: a survivors group that Jessie steered me to, and Keira's best friend, Shelley. You see, Shelley and Tyler's part in Keira's death was never made public. I only found out because Shelley came to me after Kate had her fatal heart attack. Shelley was feeling so much pain and guilt that it was literally killing her. She was down to about ninety pounds and starving herself to death despite her parents' frantic efforts to get her help. I spent weeks talking to her, convincing her that it wasn't her fault and that Keira would never want her to punish herself this way. Focusing on saving Shelley's life saved my life. I'm still involved with Jessie's group, and that too has helped."

Luce started to speak, but Stephanie interrupted her. "Wait a minute. Keira didn't just come with a message for me. She had one for you, too."

"I guess."

"You know she did. You told me all about it. What are you going to do?"

"I don't know. I really haven't had time to think."

"You told me Keira said you don't know for sure that you're going to die. Maybe from where she is, she knows something you don't."

Luce sighed. She had considered that while mulling over the strange events, but it had taken so much mental and emotional effort to come to her original decision, she wasn't sure whether she was up to revisiting it.

Stephanie set down her cup and stood. "I need to go now, Luce. You've given me so much to think about. But before I go, I want you to know that Keira fought with everything she had to live. When they found that animal, he was covered with scratches and bruises she'd given him. Believe me, if she came to you with a message, it's worth listening to."

Luce followed Stephanie to the door as she considered the words. Stephanie stopped and regarded Luce. "Well?"

"I don't know. I can't make any promises."

"But you'll think about it, right? You'll consider what my daughter said?"

Luce chuckled. "I can see where your daughter got her terrier-style debating technique."

Stephanie smiled, and for the first time Luce saw a clear resemblance to Keira. "Our first date didn't exactly go well. Would you like to try again next weekend?"

Luce blinked. "That would be great. Same place?"

Stephanie blushed and shook her head. "No. I think I left too much of a lasting impression there. How about I call you by Thursday with the time and restaurant?"

"All right. I'll look forward to it. Thank you so much for giving me a chance to explain."

As Luce closed the door behind her guest, she realized she meant it. She wanted to get to know Keira's mother better. With a bemused smile, Luce went to the answering machine and began to delete all of Jessie's messages, then she paused and pressed "repeat".

"Ms Sheppard, this is Dr. Morrow's office calling. It is urgent that we reschedule the follow-up appointment you cancelled. Please call 403-555-7993 at your earliest convenience."

Luce's finger hovered over delete. Then she picked up a pen and jotted the number down. "I'm not making any promises, Keira, but I'll think about it."

Ferron barked several times.

Luce glanced up. "What's your problem, little missie?"

Ferron looked past her.

Luce turned and caught a glimpse of something moving out of the corner of her eye, but it was gone before she could so much as blink.

An unexpected sense of peace welled up within Luce. Knowing that she had a long evening ahead and a lot of thinking to do, she returned to the kitchen for more coffee, Ferron on her heels. For the first time, she knew that whatever she chose, whatever decision she made, she wasn't making it alone.

AUTHOR'S NOTE

"To Day, my beloved pumpkin master"

BATTERIES NOT INCLUDED
by L.T. Smith

THINGS HAD BEEN HAPPENING for months. Just little things at first, nothing I could really put my finger on and say it wasn't right. Things like missing keys, an ornament turned to face the wrong way, or even new batteries dying within hours of being replaced.

Now, I'm not the kind of woman who gets spooked easily, mainly because I'm not usually the kind of woman who notices anything that is happening around her. All I seem to do is work and then work some more, and, if the mood strikes, maybe I will do a little more work.

But even I had to stop and take note of the fucked up, weird-as-shit things that were beginning to plague my everyday world.

I could deal with missing keys, cope with ornaments that appear to move or be turned around, even put up with batteries not doing their job. However, I was getting increasingly worried about other things that were beginning to manifest in my life.

October announced her arrival with heavy rain and a desperate drop in temperature. I had just finished working and was half slumped into my chair, my reading glasses falling down my nose as if to escape being overused. I'd had enough of numbers and stats, as they were beginning to blur and seemed to float and dance across the screen of my laptop.

Initially, I thought it was my imagination, thought the noise coming from above me was a remnant of me jerking awake, like most people do when they are on the cusp between sleep and the waking world.

Scraping. No, more like dragging. Fleeting, but still,

something that made me sit up and glare at the ceiling as if the answer would be written in black and white across the Artex.

I pulled my glasses off, threw them onto the table next to my laptop, and stood up a little too quickly, which made my head swim slightly.

Standing at the bottom of the stairs in the hallway, I began to lose my nerve. What if it was a burglar? An attacker? Or someone who wanted to sneak in and sneak out with my shitty jewellery, or wanted to sneak up behind me and play hide-the-sausage whilst I screamed and begged for mercy? Not the best way to describe rape, but I was trying to play it down instead of anticipating the horrors of being raped in my own home.

I backed away from the stairs and into the kitchen, my hand feeling around behind me for the bread knife I had used earlier to open a bag of crisps. I didn't want to turn my back on the staircase in case whatever was up there decided to come down.

Even as I ascended the stairs, I knew I looked like a dick. A dick wielding a ten-inch knife and hoping I was completely wrong about all the possible scenarios flitting through my head.

Click. One light on. Another click, then another, until the whole of my upstairs looked like Blackpool illuminations. I moved with the grace of Cagney or Lacey, and I mean how they would move now, twenty-five years after the show went off the air. Deep within my fucked up brain, I believed if I made enough noise, the would-be attacker or "fingersmith" would hear me and bugger off, thinking I was the size of an elephant.

Nothing was amiss. Nothing. All rooms were devoid of danger, and I slumped against the wall in relief, the knife of doom dangling from my fingers. A short laugh escaped my mouth as I mentally called myself a twat.

However, when I began to descend the stairs, another noise caught my attention. This time, it came from downstairs. What if the noise upstairs had just been a distraction to get me away from my laptop? I had confidential data exposed in what I had thought was an empty room, and now it was accessible to anyone who had the balls to shimmy in through one of my windows.

I clutched the knife, my best friend and sole protector, and decided this time I would Ninja down the stairs and surprise whatever little shit thought it was okay to break into my house.

Every creak, every groan of the wooden steps seemed to reverberate off the walls and scream, "I'm on my way! Take the computer and run!" And every time it happened, I sucked air in between my teeth and froze on the spot, my heart beating triple-time as the seconds elapsed.

It is amazing how many floorboards seem to want to make you aware that they are in need of replacing or a damned good oiling, when you most want them to stay quiet. Not just on the stairs, but right along the hallway, too.

Kitchen? Empty. Dining room? Empty. Downstairs toilet? Empty, and in need of a cleaning.

The only room left was the living room.

As I poked my head around the corner of the doorframe, I slipped my knife in front of me as if it would change colour if there was an intruder present, like my very own Orc detector. I could see my distorted reflection in the blade, although at that moment it might have actually been how my face looked—pained and distorted, with lashings of fear mixed in.

Nothing. No one. Empty.

The light from the screen of my laptop glowed like phosphorescence had seeped from within its inner workings, but even under stress, I knew that was my imagination. It was just the screen saver bubbling around and trying to alleviate my sense of impending doom by showing calmingly innocuous pictures of fish flitting across the screen.

It didn't work. Impending doom was still on the menu.

Everything was still, quiet, expectant. I didn't know why, but it was.

I moved into the room and stood next to the table, my eyes trying to pick out anything that seemed out of the ordinary. Nothing.

A click. A whirr. The disappearing screen saver was

replaced by an open Word document. Considering I'd been using Excel before I went on my reconnaissance mission to the second floor, this was a little unnerving, to say the least.

Leaning closer, I stared at the screen. There was nothing written on the page—just whiteness, and the faint colourings of Office 2010.

I moved the mouse to the exit button on the top right hand of the screen, but before I pressed the little red and white box, something else caught my eye. Right on the top line, and smack bang in the middle, sat two words that stated the document's title, as if someone had already saved it: **Ding Dong.**

What the fuck? Ding fucking dong? Who would call a document—

DING DONG!

The sound of the doorbell made me fall forward, the knife clanking against the table top.

DING DONG DING DONG!

Staggering to my feet, I tried to control my heartbeat by taking deep breaths. It wasn't working. The breaths should have been slow and deep, not like the gulping of a person who was about to be submerged underwater for an immeasurable period of time.

The rapid, shallow breathing was making me dizzy. I thought it was the influx of oxygen that made the doorway seem to waver and jiggle about.

DING DONG!

Whoever was at my front door was insistent; I gave them that. I somehow also knew that the person at the door would be able to help me in some way. How they would help was a mystery. It didn't occur to me that the person ringing my doorbell might be the bastard who was making noises and saving ridiculously-named documents on my computer.

I stumbled down the hallway, but this time not one floorboard protested. I grabbed the chain that secured the front door and fumbled while trying to release it, the links seeming to taunt me with their sly ability to elude me. There was nothing left for it—I had to drop the knife. In my state, I doubt I would have had the energy to defend myself anyway. The blade clacked onto the wooden floor and skidded towards the empty shoe rack.

Eventually the chain was undone, and so was the lock. I was having additional difficulty now. My vision was blurry, and my breathing was doing a wonderful impression of an asthmatic or someone suffering from hyperventilation.

Pulling the door back seemed to wipe me out, and I thudded into the side of it. A soft female voice started to speak, started to apologise for intruding at such a late hour, but it changed to a simple, "Are you okay?" just before I felt the solid hardness of the front doorstep meet and greet the side of my head, and my whole world went black.

꿍

When I came to, I was sprawled on the sofa in my living room, my head propped on a cushion. The room seemed odd, as if it was off kilter in some way. Pushing forward, I tried to sit up, but the pain ripped through the right side of my head and my stomach roiled in sympathy.

"Don't get up." It was the softly spoken voice I'd heard before I went arse over tit on over the threshold. "Lie back. You've had a nasty bump."

Too right. I was sure that if I concentrated a little, I could actually feel the lump still growing.

I could feel someone next to me, a presence casting a shadow over my body. Looking up, I expected to see the face of the woman who had dinged and donged my bell. But there was no one there.

"Where do you keep your plastic bags?"

Her voice drifted in from the kitchen, a distance that was way too far for her to have skittled off to in such a short span of time. I knew someone had been next to me. Knew it. I had felt the presence, sensed the shadows, been readying myself to thank the stranger for helping me get back inside the house.

But then again, I had just suffered a blow to the head after passing out due to my very own self-inflicted "Shit Yourself Up Party." I wasn't surprised that I was not in my right mind.

"Excuse me."

The voice was behind me now, and I needed to make sure that I wasn't dreaming or hallucinating. Slowly, with a great deal of pain, I turned to face the voice. If I had felt lightheaded before, it paled in comparison to how I was feeling now.

I slowly sucked air in through my teeth. Standing in front of me was one of the most beautiful women I thought I had ever seen. Her light brown hair hung to just below her shoulders, the slight curl in it turning up and caressing her throat. From where I was sitting, I couldn't make out whether her eyes were brown or green, but it didn't matter. They seemed to sparkle as they caught my gaze, and I sensed, then saw the smile that bloomed like a blush over her face—one minute it wasn't there, the next it was. It seemed to light up her whole face, made it glow, made it come alive.

"Good to see you're awake."

Her voice was gentle, and slightly husky, though the latter might have been my imagination.

I tried to sit up but slumped back onto the sofa as the effort caused pain to rip through my head again.

"Hey. Lie still. You've had a nasty bump." The nameless woman moved closer to me but stopped, as if she was unsure where her boundaries were. "I was going to fix you an ice pack, but I couldn't find anything to put the ice into."

"Bottom drawer near the fridge."

Man. I was such a charmer. Why did I always have to be so practical? Why did I have to tell her where something was so she would have to move out of my sight? Maybe because I am a knob.

I could hear the bumping of the drawers as they moved in and out, the rustle of the carrier bag, the thunk of the freezer door opening and rummaging beginning, and all the while I lay there willing her to come back so I could see her again.

With that thought came another. *Why on earth am I so intent on seeing her again? I don't do "seeing again." I do "I need this. No strings."*

"Here you go."

Even before I heard her voice, I knew she was there. It was just a feeling, although the last time I had felt her presence—had a "feeling"—I had been imagining it.

"Hold it up against the side of your head...like so." She placed the freezing cold compress on my head.

Eyes closed against the pain, I placed my hand over hers as I took over the weight of the ice bag. It was as if time stood still, as if something seemed to burrow inside of me as we touched, as if she had always been next to me in some form or another.

"How's that?"

That incomparable voice again. It had a certain timbre to it, a definite lilt. I didn't think I would ever get tired of hearing it.

"Are you okay?"

I slowly opened my eyes and looked straight into concerned hazel eyes. A light golden brown seemed to circle her pupil, and varying shades of green formed the rest of the glorious iris. Her eyes almost appeared to shimmer. Just looking into them made it difficult for me to croak out a "yes" in response to her concern.

"Do you want me to call someone?"

It was a simple question, but I couldn't speak. I just shook my head. Why didn't she break eye contact? Why did I feel as if she was absorbing me with her scrutiny?

I saw every movement on her face, every tiny nuance of expression—the shift in her mouth, the dilating of her pupils, the small tilt of her head. And all without breaking eye contact, until she did.

She blinked. Blinked again. Seemed to shiver slightly before stepping back.

Fuck. I had definitely unnerved her, as if answering the door and nearly falling on top of her whilst having a panic attack hadn't unnerved her already.

"Do you think you need it go to A and E?"

I watched her move further away and wanted to grab her hand and pull her back, pull her closer to me. Part of me knew that if she was close, we would both be safe, although I wasn't at all sure what we would be safe from. Disappointment sifted through me because I knew I couldn't pull her into my arms and feel that sense of safety. I knew that if I grabbed her, it would make me seem even madder than I undoubtedly already appeared to her. Sadly, it didn't matter; I was good at pretending I was okay. I always had been.

Gritting my teeth, I sat up and pushed back into a sitting position against the sofa cushion.

"Sorry for everything." The words left my mouth without thought or preamble. "I don't know what happened." True, for the most part. I didn't know what had happened. Still didn't.

And I still didn't know who she was.

"No. Please don't apologise." She leaned forward and briefly grabbed my hand, then released it as if she'd been burned. "I saw all the lights on and thought I'd come over and introduce myself." She stood straighter, coughed slightly, then put out her hand. "Lauren Mitchell. Your new neighbour."

My new neighbour? What happened to my old neighbour? I reached out to take her hand, hesitating slightly before I slipped my fingers around hers. "Alex Stevens."

Two words. That's all I had to say. But those two words seemed as if they were gritted out from between two sheets of sandpaper. I didn't even add a welcome to my introduction, and I wanted to kick myself for being a social misfit.

My eyes moved to our clasped hands. It seemed so natural to be holding hers in mine. But, even though the sensation of her hand in mine was divine, I summoned my manners and pulled away. I didn't want to be clingy.

"It's lovely to meet you, Alex."

See? She could do it. She could be the perfect hostess, even in my house.

Instead of completing the customary exchange, I grunted. Fucking grunted. Like a Neanderthal.

There was a brief silence, and then Lauren spoke again. "I

know the Sold sign was up for ages, but I have only just returned from abroad."

Sold sign? What happened to old Mrs Peters? Or was her name Davidson? Or Peterson?

"It worked out well, actually, as Mrs Roberts'—"

That was her name.

"…property was in probate for months, and I could wait to move in."

"She's dead! Mrs Roberts is dead?" The ice pack slid off my head and slipped down the side of the sofa.

Lauren's eyes widened at my outburst.

"But she can't be dead!" I struggled to sit up, or rather, I attempted to get up but realised I was trapped between the back of the sofa and Lauren standing in front of me.

"I'm so sorry. I thought you knew."

"Dead?" The word came out as a sob.

Lauren slipped her hands around my shoulders and drew me up into a full body hug. The feel of her warmth against me made the tears flow.

"I'm sorry. Were you two close?"

I shook my head against her chest, gripping her as if my life and my sanity depended on it.

"By all accounts, she went peacefully."

I drew back and looked into concerned hazel eyes. My mouth kept opening and closing, the words jamming in my throat, defiantly refusing to be voiced. I growled, hoping to clear the blockage. Thankfully, it worked. "I'm not crying because she's dead."

Lauren tilted her head in question.

"I'm crying because I spoke to her this morning as she was entering her house."

Not the best start to meeting someone, is it? Telling them, in no uncertain terms, that you either saw a ghost or were as nutty as a fruitcake. Trust me to do a really bad impression of the kid from *The Sixth Sense* and declare "I see dead people" to someone I had just met.

If the situation hadn't been so fucked up, I would have

laughed at Lauren's facial expression. She tried, bless her, tried to act nonchalant and dismissive, asking me was I sure I wasn't mistaken. I mean, the woman was dead. D.E.A.D. People didn't pop back from the Underworld toting a shopping bag labelled Tesco, did they?

I couldn't remember my dead neighbour's name, couldn't really remember anything much about her. Mrs Roberts, I mean. We had talked a fair number of times when she had been outside as I was coming home from work, or sometimes we would chat over the fence in the back garden. To be honest, though I had been polite, I was always in a rush to finish one job or another.

Don't get me wrong. I wasn't the kind of person who avoided my neighbours, but I wasn't the kind to put myself out to keep in touch with them, either. As I've already said, when I was not working... Actually, I was always working.

Work was my life. Everything revolved around work. I didn't really socialise, didn't really do anything but punch in numbers and solve the fiduciary problems of people who couldn't sort out their own finances.

As for relationships— you know that, too. One night stands and no strings. Family? Not really. Well, I did have, but it was too much of an effort for me to visit my two brothers and my parents.

I'm lying. It wasn't the effort as much as the anger I still harboured for them all. The way they supported my ex instead of me, saying they were not surprised she left me as I hadn't given her as much time as I should have done. What they didn't realise was that if it wasn't for me working all the hours God sent me, then I wouldn't have had what I had today.

And what I had today, I suddenly realised, actually amounted to nothing. I had material things, but I hadn't felt alive.

I attempted to stand, and Lauren shifted out of my way.

Once on my feet, I didn't know where I should go. It would be impolite to ask my new neighbour to leave, considering she had helped me get inside the house after my fall, tried to help and take care of me. She had also broken the news about my neighbour's demise. Even so, the realisation of my life being shit made me want to hole up and lick my wounds, and I couldn't really do that with someone else in the house. It was too personal, too exposing.

However, knowing I had freaked Lauren out by informing her I had seen a dead woman entering her new home earlier in the day stopped me from making another social faux pas and returning to the solitary life I'd just realised I had. Even I wasn't that clueless.

I knew what I should do, what I wanted to do, and it didn't involve sending Lauren away.

Decision made, I turned back to her. "Do you fancy a cuppa? I think we both need one."

She nodded, and as I turned to go into the kitchen, something sparkled next to my sleeping laptop and caught my eye. Something long. Something glistening. Something with a serrated edge.

I picked up the bread knife from the wooden coffee table. Might as well put it back, or I might end up losing it completely or inadvertently causing myself an injury. "Thanks for picking this up. It was its own danger zone out there."

"Picking what up?" Lauren's voice sounded strange, the kind of strange that seems to be determinedly calm but underneath the tranquil tone, emotion is raging off the scale.

"This." I waved the knife in front of her. "I dropped it at—"

"But I didn't pick it up. It was sitting there when I brought you in here."

The knife handle seemed to sear my skin, and I dropped it back onto the table. It skittered close to the edge and tottered for what seemed an interminably long time.

"Alex?" Her voice was low, and the question in the way she said my name was not questioning my identity. "What's going on?"

How could I begin to explain what the fuck was going on when I didn't have a clue myself? So, like the trooper I am, I shrugged and moved backwards towards the kitchen to fulfil my promise of tea.

Instead of taking a seat on the sofa, Lauren began to follow me. Maybe she wanted to be near me and not left all alone in my living room. Maybe it was that she could keep an eye on me if she stayed close.

Neither of us spoke whilst I filled the kettle and sorted out the mugs. Although the air should have been full of the tension of unvoiced questions, it wasn't. It was just normal.

Instead of asking if she took sugar, I held up the bag and waved it.

"Nope. Just milk, please."

I carried on, the task taking on an importance not typically associated with making tea. As long as I was busy doing something, then I wouldn't have to think about the things that had happened.

Alas, a kettle, even watched, boils eventually. We took the mugs into the dining room.

I plonked a mug in front of her and made to sit at the dining room table.

"Alex? What happened earlier? Why did you seem so terrified when you answered the door?"

"It was because you rang the bell."

Fuck. That seemed lame even to my ears. So, I prepared to explain further, but she interrupted me before I had chance to speak. Can someone be interrupted if she hasn't spoken? Who cares?

"I didn't ring your bell."

My eyes shot up to meet hers. One look at her open expression told me she was telling the truth.

Her gaze shifted away from mine. "Wait. I lied."

Hark at me and my uncanny ability to read people.

"I did press it once, but it didn't work."

I snorted. Then realised what she had said. "You're joking, right? You must have rung it at least four times." My hand was beginning to shake, and I placed the hot drink on the table before I caused myself further injury.

Lauren shook her head. "I knocked once, and you opened the door and nearly fell on top of me." Her gaze drifted upward, as if she was trying to recall something. "Wait. Let me think." Her hand moved as if ringing a doorbell, stopped, and then pantomimed knocking. "Come to think of it, I was still knocking as I heard you opening the door."

I snorted. Again. It was a new thing for me, as I never snorted at anything. Amazing what a fright, a blow to the head, finding out your dead next-door neighbour was still shopping at Tesco, and then more frights could do to a girl.

"But..."

But what? How could I dispute what she had said when "normal" seemed to be a thing of the past?

"My bell does work."

What a comeback! My bell does work?

Weirdly enough, Lauren smiled, her beautiful face morphing into something wickedly alluring. "Shall we test your assertion?"

"What?" Was I being challenged?

"It's simple. Let's ring your bell."

When I've not had the crap scared out of me, I typically would have given a very different response from the one I managed. "Sure."

A smug look materialised on my face. Considering everything that had happened, why I felt smug about hearing a DING DONG from my bell was beyond me, but my inner warrior had something to prove.

Lauren went to the front door and opened it, leaned out, and pressed the bell.

Nothing.

I nodded at her to press it again, so she did.

Still nothing.

I motioned her out of the way, then looked straight into her eyes as I pressed the button myself to prove her wrong.

Nothing.

Another press. And another. But each time there was silence, and an increasingly smug look on Lauren's face.

I pushed past her to the box on the wall. Maybe she had discharged the batteries with all her dinga ding dinging. The batteries in my house were playing up, after all.

Amazingly, I didn't come out with a string of X-rated epithets when I discovered there were no batteries in the box. It was devoid of batteries. In other words, the batteries had been taken out.

"But I..."

"That much is obvious, Alex."

"They were..."

"I know. Come on."

Her hand was warm as she took mine, or perhaps it felt warm because my hand was ice cold.

Lauren led me back to the living room and motioned for me to sit on the sofa, then she went and collected the teas before sitting next to me and handing me my cup.

Minutes passed. Long minutes that seemed like hours.

"Let me get this straight." Her voice broke through my fugue and drew me back into the moment. "You thought I rang your bell. Not a biggy. It could have been anything that made you think you heard it."

"I heard it."

Lauren's expression changed into a grimace. "But you couldn't have, Alex. No batteries, remember?"

"I heard the doorbell."

She sighed and placed her cup on the table before turning to face me again.

Despite the situation being fucked up, at that precise moment I felt a strong connection to Lauren. I had the urge to touch her face, touch her hair, trail my fingers down the firm line of her jaw. Her eyes were so beautiful, so warm and understanding, that I felt as if I had found something I had been looking for all of my life.

Stupid, I know. It should take more than an initial strong reaction and a pair of gorgeous eyes to make me feel so strongly in such a short span of time, but I did. She felt so right. Me being with her just felt so bloody right.

Then my emotions shifted again.

How could this be? I didn't do this. My life was meant to be solitary, that much I understood. The reason I knew was simple: Nothing had ever worked out for me. No one had ever been able to penetrate the solitary walls I had systematically built through years of failed relationships and my submergence into work. Eventually I gave up trying to be in a relationship and, through dedication and abstinence, I made sure it stayed that way.

I knew I was meant to be on my own. It hurt too much to keep failing at love. Offers from people at work for coffee, dinner, or a trip to the movies were always declined. So, how was it that I wanted coffee, dinner, and a trip to the movies with Lauren Mitchell? And, more importantly, was I suddenly willing to risk the pain of being emotionally exposed to someone I had just met?

Snapping out of my introspection, I realised what I had been doing. Staring. That's what. Planning my life through dating etiquette without even knowing whether the woman seated beside me, giving me a strange look, was gay.

"Are you going to answer me?" Her voice broke through my reverie, making me lean forward slightly. "And don't say you heard the doorbell. We've done that one to death."

My defensiveness snapped into action. "I wasn't going to say that." I tried to recall what she had asked me. Did she mean what had happened before I heard the doorbell, or had she asked me something else while I was previewing my life with her?

That question was on the tip of my tongue, but it didn't get the chance to be expressed.

A thunking noise came from directly above us.

Lauren's eyes met mine, "I didn't realise you had someone living here with you."

I took the cup from her hand and placed it next to mine on the table, then stood up and offered my hand to my neighbour. "I don't."

She hesitated, trying to read my expression. "Then what

was that noise?"

I pulled her up, drew her body into full contact with mine. The heat of her radiated through her clothes, and I was tantalized by the subtle scent of her perfume. Lauren was slightly taller than me, but I didn't mind tilting my head to keep looking into those hazel pools.

Our mouths were really close, and if I had any doubts before that Lauren Mitchell was gay, they dissipated like melting butter. It was too intimate a position for two women to be in unless some form of attraction was taking place. I wanted to close the gap and take her mouth with mine, claim it, taste it, devour it.

Thud!

Another sound from above, and the moment was lost.

"There must be someone upstairs. Shall we call the police?"

I shook my head and released Lauren.

"Or..." Realisation dawned on her. "...get the knife."

I shook my head again and then nodded towards the stairs in the hallway to indicate that we should investigate.

Now we were definitely Cagney and Lacey, where before, there had been just me. Moving down the hallway, we were a damned sight quieter than when I had done it alone.

The lights had been left on from my lone foray, so we didn't have to click and wait for all of the rooms to be bathed in light. Each room was as I had found it before—empty, undisturbed. Until we reached the spare room where I kept most of the stuff I classified as "don't-know-what-to-do-with-you" shit.

A box that had heretofore rested quite securely on the side table was now on the floor, its contents spilled over the carpet. It hadn't been like that when I had checked the room earlier. It had been neatly centred and nowhere near falling onto my deep shag.

Moving into the room, I immediately felt the drop in temperature. Considering that the furnace was on, the room was giving an unexpected impression of a freezer. The breath was exiting my mouth in visible puffs.

I knew Lauren and I were not the only ones in the room. I couldn't see anyone else, but I just knew we were being watched.

"What's in...or was in the box?"

Lauren's voice was a whisper, but it boomed at the side of my head, and I jumped back and slammed into her. I heard a distinct "Oomph" at the contact and turned to apologise.

As I opened my mouth, I stopped. Someone else had spoken, someone other than either of us. I didn't understand what the voice said, but I had definitely heard a voice coming from behind me.

The hairs on the back of my neck stood to attention, soldiers standing sentry to ward off something I couldn't see.

"Did you..." Lauren's voice was shaking.

I understood what she was trying to say. I grimaced as I took her hand in mine. The heat of her skin was almost scorching, maybe because the room was so cold. I wanted to run, wanted to grab Lauren and race down the stairs and out into the street. But that wouldn't serve any purpose. I would have to come back inside later, and when that happened, I wouldn't have my wingman with me.

It was time to take action, time to get a spine and move into the room and find out what the fuck was happening, find out who was fucking about with my box and whispering unintelligible epithets—probably of doom and demise—into my ear.

I made my decision. "You can stay here if you want." Deep down I was secretly hoping Lauren would tell me to get out of the way so that she could be the lead investigator. After all, she was the taller.

Instead, she gripped my fingers more tightly, gave me a wan smile, and nodded for me to proceed.

To say I was scared would have been redundant. My eyes had joined in on the fear front, my vision blurring as though I was wearing beer goggles. I blinked rapidly, hoping to clear the haze, but they were having none of it. Perhaps they thought the less I could see, the better it would be. This was a feeling I didn't really want. If I was going to confront my attacker, I wanted to see him, or her, up close. Wanted to see every line and curve of the face of the one who would write "Fin" on my life.

One step. Two. Make that three. The box hadn't moved. It lay there like a wounded casualty, its guts hanging out. Another step…then another.

Lauren was still hanging on to my hand; the coldness of the room sealed our breath into pockets in front of us.

"Alex?"

Lauren's voice sounded different, and I felt badly about making her come into the room with me.

"Alex?"

"Yes?" I stopped and looked back at her.

She looked back at me. "What?"

How come her voice sounded different when I was facing her?

"You said my name."

Lauren pursed her lips. "No I didn't. I heard you speak, but couldn't make out what you were saying."

She was either winding me up or—

"Allllleeeeeex!"

An insistent whisper sounded in my left ear, and I jumped back, Lauren's hand gripped firmly in mine.

"Who? What? Fuck!"

My heart hammered in my chest, and I knew the blood in my veins was pumping too fast to be classified as healthy. Without thought, I grabbed onto Lauren and drew her up beside me. This was not to use her as a human shield; it was more to protect her. Or so I hoped she would believe.

The light went off.

I couldn't tell you which of us screamed the loudest, but I know for a fact that I was a contender. Actually, I think I out-vocalized Lauren when the door to the bedroom slammed shut.

Lauren grabbed on to me, and I grabbed on to her. We gripped. We shook. We couldn't see a damned thing. And we couldn't seem to move. Maybe it was fear, maybe it was comfort, but we stayed locked together as if our conjoined bodies would stave off whatever had turned the lights off and shut us in the room.

Ding Dong!

What the fuck? The doorbell was ringing. The fucking doorbell was ringing. Without batteries. Without fucking batteries. If I'd thought I was losing my marbles before, now I was sure of it.

A sound from the far side of the room seemed amplified over the wild beating of my heart. A scraping, a dragging, a moving of something that wasn't being done by either Lauren or me.

Ding Dong Ding Dong!

I hated bells. Hated them. Especially haunted ones—ones that had a life and a purpose of their own and would display this fact willy nilly.

The scraping and dragging sounds were moving closer to where we were standing.

Lauren tightened her arms around me, and if I hadn't been truly petrified, I would have enjoyed the contact.

As cold as the temperature in the room was already, I felt it drop even further. The
column of air in front of us should have been frozen.

I had the distinct feeling that someone was standing directly in the pillar of space where the icy draught was situated. And that someone was looking at us. Someone we couldn't see, could only feel was looking straight at us...and waiting.

"You need her."

It wasn't Lauren, and it wasn't me. It wasn't anything but a voice and a sensation of cold.

I moved away from Lauren, pushed her behind me to protect her, her hands trying to pull me back and into her embrace, as if she wanted to guard me instead.

"Need her."

That voice. I knew it, didn't I? Knew the quietness of it, knew the timbre. I also knew that voice would not hurt me. It couldn't. Reason? The person who belonged with that voice was dead.

Instead of screaming again, or running for the hills, I smiled into the dark, hoping my smile was aimed toward the presence. "Mrs Roberts?" I asked, my voice holding a semblance of surety.

The small laugh was the same kind of laugh she would make when she saw me trying to tame my garden.

"Need her."

Before I could ask who needed whom, the light flicked back on. There was nothing standing in front of us—no Mrs Roberts, no nothing.

Lauren's death grip relaxed slightly, but she tensed again as the bedroom door eased open.

Slowly, I pulled away from her. The temperature in the room returned to normal, but I felt the chill as my body lost contact with the woman I had been holding.

Ding Dong

What was the matter with technology these days? How could the bell be ringing when it shouldn't?

Ding

It sounded as if the batteries were dying. That was nothing new in my house, but there hadn't been any batteries in the bell in the first place.

"Are you going to get that?"

I looked into Lauren's eyes, fully expecting her to smile or otherwise indicate she was pulling my leg. But it was obvious by the bewildered expression on her face that she meant it.

I shrugged my shoulders nonchalantly. There would be nothing there, so why would I—

Do…ng

It was another instance of wanting to prove her wrong that made me say, "Come on. Let's check it out, shall we?"

As I moved away, Lauren pulled me back and pointed.

"Look."

I did.

There, sitting innocuously on the table, was the box. All the contents were inside it, not splayed over the floor as they had been before the blackout. Even more eerie was that the box was sealed up, as if it had been that way forever.

Once again, I shrugged. At that point, there was not much else that would have surprised me.

Approaching the front door, I said, "Don't be upset if there is only fresh air outside. Or the ghost of Christmas Past." I grinned at my attempted joke, even though it was shit one.

I opened the door and saw a man standing on the stoop.

After all that had happened prior to that moment, seeing a real live human being standing on my doorstep scared the crap out of me. I screamed.

Because I screamed, Lauren joined in—although I don't think she knew why, that it was probably a chain reaction.

The man standing outside screamed, too, and then we all screamed again.

My poor heart. I didn't think it could take any more.

The man turned out to be Mrs Roberts' son, who had come by his mother's house to say hello to Lauren. Upon finding her house empty and her front door open, he had been worried about leaving her house so vulnerable to burglars. Seeing all my lights on, he had come around to inquire if I had seen my new neighbour, and if not, to ask if I could keep an eye on her house. When he had been confronted by two screaming women, he had reacted like most people would in that situation.

By way of apology, I invited him in for a cuppa. It was the least I could do after scaring the crap out of him.

Whilst I was sorting out the tea, Lauren went back to her house to lock the door. I wanted to tell her that it didn't matter, since it appeared that whatever was out to get us could apparently drift through walls, but I thought better of it. No point in shitting her up even more.

Mr Roberts didn't stay long. He just made some polite

conversation and made to leave.

As he was exiting the door, he turned back. "By the way, thought I'd let you know—your bell doesn't work."

I smiled at him. "Really?" I wasn't being sarcastic, but what was the point in trying to explain.

"It's probably just the batteries," he said, and then he was gone.

I closed the door and turned to look at Lauren. She was leaning against the wall, looking absolutely breath-taking.

I slowly closed the small distance between us. My eyes flickered over her face, absorbing the beauty of Lauren Mitchell.

"She was right, you know." The words effortlessly left my lips.

I saw Lauren take in a deep breath before asking, "About?"

I leaned forward, my lips mere millimetres from hers. The air was electric, expectant. I waited for her to move away, to tell me this was not what she wanted, but the rejection didn't come.

"I do need you."

As our lips met for the very first time, the bells I heard were not coming from my doorbell.

LOST AND FOUND
by Emma Weimann

S HE WAS RUNNING AS FAST as she could.
As if on purpose, branches hit her face, her body,—
and then morphed into the gloating face of her ex before
transforming back into branches.

Something grabbed Laura from behind.

She fought against the pull and got free. She knew that she
would never be able to leave this place if she didn't escape
now. Ignoring the stitch in her side, she kept on running—
through the darkness, towards safety.

A flash. A blinding light.

She found herself in a clearing.

Voices echoed from behind her. Lights, like fireflies but
fast as wasps, swarmed around her, making a buzzing noise
that grated on her shaken nerves. What were these things?

Her brother's voice rang in her head, "Once a loser, always
a loser."

She turned her head and saw a mound to her left. Maybe
she could hide behind it. Running in that direction, she tripped
over something and fell. Pain lanced through her knees.

Her brother and her ex appeared as foggy figures in front
of her. They were laughing like mad.

For a split second, Laura thought about staying on the
ground where she was, giving up.

The voices behind her were closer now. They were like
wolves hunting their prey, waiting until she was exhausted and
made a mistake that would cost her life—or her soul.

She struggled to her feet and skirted around the foggy
shadows of her brother and her ex.

An almost-human scream of pain, anguish, and hate echoed

from behind her.

Laura sat bolt upright, her breathing ragged and her limbs trapped in the tangled sheets. *Shit. A dream.* It had been another one of her stupid nightmares.

"Damn." She massaged her temples with trembling fingers. Her goal for this vacation had been to gain a new perspective on her life, not to have to force herself awake every night to escape from a nightmare. And what stupid nightmares they were. *Hunted by otherworldly beings in a forest. God, that is really ridiculous.* She would have understood if the nightmare had been about her ex hunting her, or if it had started with the image of her ex and her brother in bed. Either of those would understandably be the stuff worthy of nightmares. But trees? And strange creatures?

Laura's gaze flitted to Oz.

Her Boston Terrier happily snored away on the other side of the bed, his little feet moving like those of a nervous boxer in the ring.

I wonder what he is dreaming about.

Laura rubbed her eyes and yawned. *Maybe coming here wasn't such a good idea.* As a child, she had spent every summer at her grandparents' place. Back then, that had meant eight blissful weeks of freedom. After her grandparents' deaths, many years earlier, she had turned the old cottage into a holiday retreat. This was Laura's first extended visit—other than the two short stays while she oversaw the work of the handyman who had done the repairs. In the interim, she had been renting out the place to tourists. But so far, Laura's time here had been anything but relaxing. *What I wouldn't give for one night of undisturbed sleep.*

With a sigh, she looked at the clock on the bedside table. *Four a.m. Shit. Way too early to get up, and impossible to go back to sleep.*

She selected a book from the pile on her nightstand. Maybe reading would make her sleepy.

One could always hope.

❧

"You just wait here." Laura patted Oz on the head.

He threw a glare at her that could have killed a small dog, but had little effect on Laura.

"I'll be back in a few minutes."

He snorted.

"I've run out of coffee at the cabin, Oz, and you know I crave coffee as much as you need your dog treats. You really want me to have enough coffee, or I will be as unbearable as you are."

Oz shuffled around in the backseat until his butt was pointed toward Laura.

She shook her head. He couldn't have made a clearer statement. Sometimes she wondered whether getting a cat would have been the better choice.

"Diva."

Sighing, Laura closed the car door and crossed the street. There had always been just one all-inclusive shop in the god-forsaken town, and it looked to be as old as Methuselah. *It hasn't changed since I was last here. And that was more than fifteen years ago.*

When she was a child, this had been the place her grandfather would take her to buy penny chews. From time to time, she was also allowed to pick two sugar mice, but only if she promised not to tell her Granny.

A smile crept over Laura's face. Her grandmother had always known without Laura ever telling her. Ms. Gunner, the shop owner, had been Granny's best friend, but Granny had never mentioned anything about the sugar mice—until the day Laura had received her cryptic last letter.

Laura kicked a pebble across the sidewalk.

To this day, she had no idea what had happened that had made her parents forbid her to visit this place, and her grandparents, anymore. When it came to that last summer, there was a black hole in Laura's memory. Both her parents and her grandparents had kept mum whenever Laura asked questions. She believed that her grandparents had been strictly admonished to do so.

Sounds of children's laughter echoed through the street, and Laura looked in the direction from whence the noise was coming.

A horde of children appeared from around the corner, hauling a cart of carved pumpkins along the street. They disappeared into a driveway and out of sight.

It's Halloween. She had totally forgotten. *I should buy some chocolate bars. Just in case.* She had no idea whether children would come up to the holiday cottage, but it was always best to be prepared.

With a grin on her face, she stepped up to the shop's door. As she reached for the knob, the door opened.

A tall woman with bright red hair smiled at her. "Hello."

Laura returned the smile and the greeting.

The stranger stepped around her and walked away, her long red hair blowing around her shoulders as if in a shampoo commercial.

Strange. There is no wind. Laura's eyes wandered down and landed on the woman's ass. An ass that was hugged by tight-fitting leather trousers. Laura grinned. *Nice.*

The woman turned and winked at Laura, then continued on her way.

Shit. Laura hid her face behind her hands. *Caught ogling the woman's ass.* She couldn't help smiling. *Well, I guess that just shows that I'm still alive.*

She turned and opened the door to the shop, and stepped into the very same dimly lit room that she remembered from her childhood. *Wow.* Timber shelves filled with tea, sugar, bread, peach cocktails, pear halves, baked beans, and Brillo pads lined the walls, hardly leaving enough space to walk around. *I should have brought my camera.* Penny chews were lined up next to the cash till. She took a step closer. *Sugar mice. I can't believe it.* Her mouth watered. *Seventy-five pence a piece. I guess I could afford a few of them.* She had no idea how much they had cost back when she came into the store with her grandpa. That memory was as fuzzy as many of her memories when it came to the time she'd spent at her grandparents'.

Laura's eyes fell on a chair in the corner. She blinked. Now that one, she remembered. Ms. Gunner's old rocking chair. And it stood in the exact same corner as it had back then.

Footsteps approached from behind the curtain.

Ms. Gunner? Laura held her breath.

An elderly man appeared—white hair, glasses like the bottoms of jam jars, and a face like a potato sack. "Are ya okay?"

Disappointment spread inside Laura. For an instant she had hoped that it would be Ms. Gunner, and that she would greet Laura like she had when Laura was a child. "Yes, thank you. I'm just doing some shopping."

"All right, dear." He winked at her. "Let me know if you need any help."

Laura rubbed the bridge of her nose. "I wonder...do you know Ms. Gunner?"

He flashed a bright smile. "Oh yes. Sure do. She was my sister, wasn't she?"

Was? Laura swallowed around the lump in her throat. "So, she's not alive?"

"No, dear. She died four years ago. She was an old lady."

Laura took a deep breath. He was right. Ms. Gunner had been a few years older than Laura's Granny. "Yes, she was."

"Did you know her?"

"Yes. She was a very good friend of my grandmother's."

"Right." He squinted at her. "I don't remember your face."

Neither had she remembered his. "I'm Laura Sullivan. Picture me a bit smaller, blond and with pigtails."

"Laura Sullivan. Sure. Little Laura. You always had an eye on the sugar mice, didn't ya?"

Wow. "And you are...?"

"Young Gunner." He winked at her again.

Of course. Ms. Gunner's younger brother. The troublemaker. "Yes, I do remember you. You had that hellion of a motorbike."

He grinned. "Still do. Still do. But I can't drive it anymore. Damned bones." He patted his hip. "So, what are you here for? Haven't seen you in ages."

I guess being half blind is another reason for not driving anymore. "I took a few days off work and am staying at my grandparents' place."

A phone rang somewhere in the back, and he cleared his throat. "Ah, Laura, I have to take this." He waved his hand in the air. "Take a look around. I'll be back in a jiffy."

It didn't take Laura long to find the coffee section—one brand of instant coffee on the shelf. *Great. Haven't had instant coffee in years and never planned to drink it again.* But she remembered that her grandparents had either served tea or instant coffee. *Guess it's a generation thing.* Should she buy it, or should she ask Young Gunner if he had real coffee hidden away somewhere? *Young Gunner.* She snorted. *Boy, did he drive his sister and my Granny crazy.* But she also remembered that he had been lots of fun, and he'd been kind to the children.

Just as she was about to put a jar of instant coffee into the shopping basket, her mobile phone rang. Laura checked the number and groaned. *Do I really want to talk to her?* The immediate answer was a clear "no." Four hours of sleep didn't support enough energy for this call. *On the other hand...* She had expected the phone call. *Get it over and done with.*

"Yes?"

"It's me, honey."

"Hi, Mum."

"I've tried to reach you several times."

How are you doing, Laura? Lousy, thank you, Mother. She cleared her throat. "I don't get a line connection at the cottage. This is the outback here."

"I really don't get why you have to stay at that place."

Sure. Make the cottage sound like a waste dump. "Well, it's a nice quiet place." Laura cradled the mobile to her ear while adding a few bars of chocolate to her basket. If no children turned up tonight, she would eat the candy herself. No point in wasting perfectly good chocolate.

"Well, I guess you're entitled to your opinion. But sweetheart, when are you coming home?"

When my brother has moved to the moon, and my former girlfriend—who I now call slut—with him. "I don't know."

"That's no answer."

Laura rolled her eyes. She laid a packet of spaghetti next to the chocolate bars. "How is Kevin doing?"

"He is so sorry, Laura. I wish you would talk to him."

Yeah, great. Love to. With a gun in my hand. "Sure. I bet he's sorry…that I interrupted them having sex in our bed." Laura did not regret the bitterness in her own voice.

"Your girlfriend seduced him."

That sounded more like the manipulative bitch her mother usually was. Laura groaned. "Sure, Mom. Talk to you in a few days." She broke off the connection and put her mobile phone back in her bag. A pang of loneliness exploded in her chest. *My brother has sex with my girlfriend, and my parents are worried about him.* Tears welled in her eyes. *Shit. Life really sucks.* The pain of betrayal hadn't diminished at all. It was festering deep inside her.

She added two bags of crisps, more chocolate, and a rather dusty looking packet of tea to her basket before she went to the counter.

Mr. Gunner greeted her with a smile. "There you are. Look. I found a little package with your name on it a while ago. My sister wanted you to have it, but I didn't have your address to forward it. Tell you the truth, I nearly forgot about it."

A small jewelry box lay in his palm. It was made of red leather and looked antique.

"What is this?"

He shook his head. "I have no idea. But my sister wanted me to give it to you."

Her brow furrowed. "When was that?"

Mr. Gunner broke eye contact. "It's been a while."

Wow. She carefully took the box from his hand. It felt as old as it looked—rough, and broken in places, but in a dark red leather that made her imagine it held the most expensive jewelry inside. A shiver went down Laura's spine. *She wouldn't pass on diamonds, silly.* Laura carefully opened the box. A light brown pendant in the shape of a shark's tooth lay inside. It hung from a leather string. *Nope. Neither diamonds nor gold.*

She took the pendant out of the box and rubbed her thumb across it. "This is wood, right?"

"Looks like it. But I've never seen it before. Strange."

The pendant was smooth, as if someone had worn it for a long time. "So, you never saw your sister wear it?"

He shook his head. "No. Never."

"Is there a letter or a card? Something?"

"No, sorry. Just the box, and the Post-it note with your name on it."

This wasn't at all the kind of jewelry she was into. *Wood. This is really weird.* On the other hand, it was just plain nice of Ms. Gunner to leave her something to remember her by.

Laura put the pendant back in its box. "Thank you very much."

"You're welcome, dear. Now, let's see what you've got." He pointed at her shopping basket.

"Oh, right. Say, do you have real coffee? I only found instant on your shelf."

He tilted his head. "What's wrong with instant?"

Laura groaned inside. She really needed to get back to civilization sooner rather than later, or she would go insane. There was only one short-term solution. "I'll also take ten sugar mice, please."

At night, the cottage was as quiet as a graveyard. Only the occasional creak of the wooden beams stretching and working, and Oz's snoring, broke the silence.

Laura sniggered. Most of the time he was a joy, in his own grumpy way, but his snores certainly could wake the dead.

I need a cuppa. She went into the kitchen and put the kettle on the stove. It was still her grandmother's orange steel teakettle—born in the 70s, and so ugly that it bordered on being cute. She had not bothered to replace it when she had inherited the cottage.

It wasn't long before the kettle whistled—a sound that brought back memories. Laura wouldn't have been surprised to see her grandmother come around the corner and demand a cup of tea for herself. *But that is not going to happen.*

She opened the tea she had bought and put some of it into one of her grandmother's old flowery Wedgwood mugs, and then poured water in over it.

Noise from outside attracted Laura's attention and drew her to the window. She saw birds darting across the lawn in their search for worms or whatever else they hunted for dinner.

Her gaze shifted to the forest, and a shiver ran down her spine. Ever since she had arrived, she hadn't been able to shake the feeling that the forest was creeping ever closer to the cottage. And sometimes she felt as if she was being observed. That was impossible; she knew that. Still, something stirred inside her every time she looked at the trees.

Closing her eyes, she inhaled the scented steam that swirled up out of the mug. There was nothing better than a cuppa to put everything in life right again. If one was British. She took a sip. With a sigh, she sat down on the sofa in the living room.

This piece of furniture was new, but most of the other stuff hadn't been replaced. Laura carefully set the cup of tea down on a coaster near the open box that contained Ms. Gunner's carved pendant. She caressed the old oak table her grandfather had brought back from an auction years and years ago. Then she reached over and picked up the unexpected gift.

What a strange thing it was. Laura stroked the wood with her thumb. She had no idea what kind of wood it was. She turned it around and found two black stones embedded in the back. Maybe the pendant had been handmade by a local artisan in this part of rural Ireland.

Laura put the pendant around her neck. The wood felt cold against her skin. She would wear it, at least for a while. Maybe it would help bring back some good memories, maybe even some of the lost ones of the childhood she had spent here.

With a deep sigh, she closed her eyes and concentrated on the silence surrounding her. The old grandfather clock in the corner set the pace of time inside the cottage. Its tick-tock was soothing and helped her relax.

Tranquility, contentment… things she found so hard to come by lately. Images of her girlfriend in bed with her brother flashed into her mind. *Shit.* It had been over a month since the incident. This was the one thing she didn't want to think about. She knew that at some point she would have to, but not now. She needed a break.

Oz was the only constant at her side and never—*Oz.*

It was too quiet.

"Oz?" *Where is the little bugger?*

She hurried into the bedroom. His favorite spot in the corner was empty. Knees trembling, she went through all the other rooms in the cottage.

No Oz.

Then she noticed the door to the garden was open slightly.

"Shit. No."

Oz was gone.

She went outside and called his name, scaring off the few birds that were still hunting for their dinner.

Laura looked at her watch. Nearly six p.m. Damned dog. And damn herself. Why had she left the back door open? Stupid. Totally stupid. Oz was new to the cottage and its surroundings, and he was most certainly no tracking dog. He could get lost in the living room. So why had the little bugger even left the cottage?

Laura went back inside. She had to find Oz before something else found him first. She grabbed the torch and her jacket. *And when I find him, I will bring him back and tie him up like a rolled pork roast. Damn dog.*

She searched the area around her cottage and the other holiday cottage that stood dark and empty at the end of the street.

No Oz.

The next place on her search list was the small barn in the nearby field. The light of her torch scared off several animals, including one very pissed off barn owl, but Oz was not there.

She had to try one last time to get him to come. "Oz?"

Laura waited.

There was only the sighing of the wind, caressing the twigs in the nearby tree.

Laura stared up. *What a peaceful night.* Clouds blanketed the stars and the moon. It was chilly but not too cold. *It's almost magical.*

Her gaze dropped to the forest that appeared like a dark cloud in front of her. *He has to be in the forest.* She looked at her watch. Nearly seven p.m.

Laura's shoulders sagged. She just knew that Oz was stupid enough to wander off into the woods filled with predators that would love to have him for a midnight snack. She shook her head at the thought; her imagination was running wild. Sure there were foxes, squirrels, skunks, and rats, as well as the occasional owl, but would they actually go after a Boston Terrier?

Taking several deep breaths, she walked toward the forest until she reached its frayed edge. Laura wiped her clammy hands on her jeans. Her throat constricted at the thought of entering this foreboding place. But what if Oz was in there? She had to find him.

She made a tentative start into the forest's dense darkness and then, after a few steps, stood still. Everything around her was grey or black. No light was finding its way through the canopy.

The longer she stared at the trees, the more she was convinced that there were faces staring back at her, which was impossible. It would take a moment for the faces to turn back into trees and bushes, and then everything would be perfectly all right again.

A twig snapped nearby.

A chill fell around her.

Laura pressed her hand against her stomach to suppress the sourness surging inside her. *There are no otherworldly creatures living in the forest.* "Come on, get your act together." The darkness swallowed her voice like a black hole.

Determined to find her stupid dog, she followed a narrow path, climbed over a storm-felled tree that lay across the little path, and shouted, "Oz?"

Nothing.

She continued along the faint path, carefully listening to the sounds around her. Laura drew a ragged breath and glanced over her shoulder. Was someone following her? She shook her head. *I've watched too many scary movies.*

Still, she couldn't shake off the feeling that the trees were observing her every step with their knothole-eyes.

Everything around her was so dark that the torch's beam only lighted what it hit directly. *This is not working. How am I supposed to find my dog in this pitch black forest?* She would give it another ten minutes or so, and then she would have to go home and come back in the morning. "Oz?"

She bit her lip as she listened intently. The only thing she heard was the creak of boughs rubbing against each other in the wind.

And then, a howl.

Laura's heart nearly jumped out of her throat. *What the fuck?* There were no wolves in this forest. *Maybe a wild dog. Shit.*

Laura cleared her throat and tried to sound stern and commanding. "Oz? Come here."

The wind suddenly sounded like voices whispering.

She shuddered.

Tendrils of fog glided through the trees.

Where is this fog coming from? What is this?

Lights appeared out of the fog and swarmed towards her as fast as wasps—like in her dream. Fear wrapped its tentacles around Laura's heart, and she could barely breathe.

Voices whispered, "A human. She is back." Excited buzzing filled the air like the tuning of the orchestra before a performance. "Let us taste her."

Something bit Laura's hand and then her nose. Pain shot through her. "Leave me alone."

Laughter bubbled up around her; more lights appeared from the fog.

She had to get away.

Laura turned around and started to run.

As if on purpose, branches hit her face, her body.

Something grabbed her from behind.

She fought against the pull and got free, able to run again.

Voices echoed from behind her. Lights, like fireflies, but fast as wasps swarmed around her.

She tripped over something and fell. Pain shot through her knees.

Bites in her hand and on her face urged her to her feet.

A shape emerged from the darkness as if exuded from it. Glowing eyes, like those she'd seen in the monster movie a few nights ago, homed in on her.

Laura wanted to run, but her feet seemed to have taken root in the ground.

"Fear not. You are under my protection."

The stranger's voice was warm, promising shelter like the shade of a tree on a hot summer day. Laura's heart hammered in her chest. She didn't dare to hope that she was safe.

A smaller shadow appeared next to the larger one.

Within a split second, the darkness around her lifted, as if someone had turned on a low light.

Laura couldn't believe her eyes. The small shadow was her missing dog, who looked none the worse for his adventure. "Oz?"

He barked twice, but didn't move away from the female stranger.

An angry buzzing sound emerged from the swarm of glowworms.

The female took a step towards the swarm, her hands balled into fists. "No, you can't have her."

Laura couldn't believe her eyes. *This is the woman from the shop.*

The swarm buzzed like mad. Their color changed from a dark yellow to a bright red, and then a dark green. Then they were gone. Vanished. Disappeared, as if they had never been. Only the painful bites on Laura's hands and face remained as proof of their existence.

Laura couldn't believe her eyes. Her thoughts were tumbling around like fleas on drugs. She didn't know what to do, didn't understand what had just happened. *Where did the insects vanish to? Who is the stranger? What is up with Oz?* However, one thing she knew for sure—she had to get the hell out of there. Back to the safety of the cottage.

The stranger's brow furrowed. "Are you hurt?"

"No, I'm not hurt. Thank you for taking care of Oz. We'd better get home now."

"It is Samhain. You can't just wander around out here on your own. No human is safe in this forest tonight."

No human? *Is she mentally ill?* Laura plastered a smile on her face and took a step back. "The crazy insects are gone, I'd better leave now. Come here, Oz."

Oz whined and stared unhappily at her, not leaving the stranger's side.

Traitor. Torn between staying with her crazy ass dog and leaving this place as fast as she could, Laura took another hesitant step backwards, hoping that Oz would follow. "Come on, Oz."

"Don't. No further." There was urgency in the stranger's voice.

Laura's heart hammered with a staccato beat. This woman was obviously crazy. She needed something to defend herself with. Laura took another step backwards and grabbed the branch of the tree to her right, trying to break it off to use as a weapon.

"Don't hurt the tree."

She is totally batshit crazy and *a tree hugger.*

Rough bark bit into Laura's hand as the branch snapped away from its trunk.

What—?

She turned her head and looked at a dark, misty form.

"You're one of the tree killers, aren't you?" The voice dripped with danger. "I will destroy you."

This is a nightmare. I need to wake up. Laura pinched the skin on her hand. The pain didn't help. She was still in the forest and not in her bed. This was the grandmother of all her nightmares—being unable to wake up.

"Leave her alone, little dryad. We won't harm you." The female stranger's voice was gentle.

"You won't, but she will." He sounded like an angry child.

"No, she won't. I give you my word."

"I will hold you to it, Morgan. If she hurts us again, I will kill her."

Morgan bowed her head. "As is your right. But it won't happen."

"See to it." The misty form morphed into the tree…and was gone. Vanished. Like the insects earlier.

For the first time in her life, Laura wondered whether fainting was a solution. *Am I crazy?*

Morgan's voice drew Laura out of her thoughts, "Come with me. We need to get you to safety."

Laura shook her head. No way was she going with this woman.

"Please, Laura."

For a second, Laura wondered when she had told Morgan her name. *Probably earlier.* "I can't. I don't know you. I want to go home right now or wake up in my own bed, if this is a dream."

Morgan smiled softly. "I'm sorry, but you can't. You have to follow me. The only thing allowed to wander is your gaze. And don't stray more than two steps away from me… no matter what."

Laura swallowed hard. "This isn't a dream?"

"No, it isn't." Morgan turned around and began to walk away. "Come on," she called over her shoulder. "You need to stay close."

Laura watched in fascination as Oz kept glued to Morgan's

side like gum to a shoe. *Maybe he knows best.*

Against her better judgment, she followed them. She stumbled over a branch lying on the ground, then struggled to keep up with Morgan and Oz, who were hurrying along as if something was on their heels.

Focusing on the ground, and on Morgan's lead, Laura tried to digest what had just happened: a swarm of aggressive nocturnal insects had cornered and bitten her before vanishing as if they had been beamed away. Then a shadowy "being" had threatened her and disappeared into a tree. *Maybe there was something in the tea I had. Maybe I'm drugged.*

That had to be it. Who knew how long the packet of tea had stood in the shop. She hadn't even bothered to check the expiration date. *Or maybe someone mixed some kind of drug with the tea leaves.* Anything was possible. *But what am I supposed to do? Run after my imaginary savior with the nice ass, or stay where I am and hope to wake up soon?*

She rubbed her hands over her face. *And where is that light coming from?* She didn't understand why everything around Morgan was bathed in the soft light that helped Laura to avoid falling over the debris on the ground.

Laura heard something rustling in the bushes to her right, and her throat went dry. *Come on. There are lots of small animals around. No point in shitting your pants at every sound.*

"Laura, you have to stay close by my side." Morgan appeared next to Laura. "Give me your hand, please."

Laura stared at the outstretched hand. "I don't know—"

A covey of birds burst out of the bushes.

And then something else moved out of hiding, something darker than darkness and blacker than night.

Morgan grabbed Laura's hand and drew her to her side. "Don't move."

The dark form pierced the darkness surrounding it.

For a moment, Laura had the impression that even the bushes and trees were trying to lean away from it. Whatever it was.

It came closer.

Laura heard the "something" sniff. Her hairs stood on end.

"She's mine," Morgan said in a calm but determined voice.

It growled.

Laura pressed close against Morgan's body. An unfamiliar tingle shot through Laura, like electricity, but the pleasant kind.

With a last growl, the darkness moved away from them— slowly, but steadily, until it disappeared from sight.

"It's okay. It won't bother you anymore." Morgan stepped away.

An unexplainable emptiness echoed through Laura. Having Morgan's body pressed against hers had made her feel safe.

"We better hurry. This forest is the Gathering Place tonight. We'll be safe in my home." Morgan turned around and began to walk even more rapidly than before.

Gathering Place? Laura hurried after Morgan, eyes focused on her ass. Laura shook her head, hoping to clear it. *Get a grip.* "What was that?"

"What was what?"

"That…thing."

"You don't want to know."

If Laura hadn't been forced to put all her energy and focus into not stumbling over branches or slipping on whatever kind of slime was partially covering the ground, she would have engaged in a discussion with Morgan about who decided what she needed or wanted to know.

"We're nearly there."

Oz's bark sounded happy.

Seconds later, they left the trees behind and Laura found herself in a clearing.

"Just a few more steps."

Laura looked down. Soft cushions of green and brown mosses covered the ground.

From out of nowhere, lights were dancing around them.

Oz whined.

Not again. Laura wrapped her arms around herself, panic racing through her.

Morgan laughed and held out her hand. One of the lights

came closer and landed on one of her fingers.

Giggles like the sound of small bells filled the air.

Laura breathed a sigh of relief. *All right. So these are not dangerous.*

The smell of strawberries wafted through the air.

Suddenly all the other lights danced so close around them that Laura was able to make out human-like faces. These weren't butterflies. *Tinker Bell. They look like Tinker Bell.*

"Pay attention, little sisters. The Hunters are out tonight." Morgan's voice was composed but serious.

Tinker Bell Number One took off from Morgan's finger, flew to her cheek and gave her a kiss.

A growl climbed up Laura's throat. Surprised, she pressed a hand over her mouth.

Morgan shot her an amused glance.

The butterfly thingy laughed before joining the other Tinker Bells. They flew away, slowly disappearing from sight.

Once again, the air smelled only of night and danger.

No more strawberries. And no more stupid behaviour. She had no idea where the growl, the possessiveness regarding Morgan, had come from. Laura turned to Morgan. "Who are you?"

"I would have thought that your question would be 'what are those'?" Morgan grinned, and a gap was visible between her two front teeth.

Where have I seen that toothy grin before? Something was nibbling at Laura's memory, but she couldn't put her finger on it. The only thing she knew was that it was a pleasant thought, a memory that was as warm and soft as Morgan's touch had been.

"Come. This is my home."

Morgan made her way towards a mound that Laura hadn't noticed. Laura followed, as did Oz, who had left Morgan's side and now walked next to Laura. She looked down at him. "You're a little traitor."

He whined, but stayed at her side.

"Finally." Morgan sounded relieved. Without further ado, she bent down, got on her knees, and crawled into an opening in the ground.

"You have to be kidding me." Laura shook her head. "I'm not crawling into this…this…"

Oz disappeared into the small opening, and Laura was left standing outside.

Alone.

A branch snapped somewhere nearby.

"Shit. Shit. Shit." She squinted out into the darkness.

"Come, Laura." Morgan's voice issued from inside the mound.

"Oh, damn. I hate this day." Swearing, Laura got to her knees and crawled through the opening. The heavy scent of ferns and moss welcomed her to the other side.

Slowly, she stood up and looked around. *This is amazing.* This place was really nice—for a mound. The ceiling was much higher than she had expected. It was only one room, but somehow airy and nice. And clean.

Candles flickered on a nearby table and on several stones that looked as if they had been strategically placed for optimum lighting. Smooth moss covered the ground. *Like a carpet.* In the back of the room was a bed. Not huge, by any means, but it looked very comfortable. *A home in a mound. This is surreal. It's like a Hobbit home.*

Oz lay curled up as if everything was totally all right and this was just the place to be.

Maybe I should trust his instincts. But she couldn't. She had to find out what had happened out in the forest. And who Morgan was.

Laura's eyes assessed her hostess. Long, red hair. She was taller than Laura. Morgan's shirt, as well as her trousers, shimmered a greenish-brown that seemed to change patterns whenever she moved. And the trousers did fit tightly. Over a really great ass. *She's a good looking woman. Hot, in a butch kind of way.*

Laura wanted to kick herself. Why was she suddenly thinking of Morgan as the hottest, toughest thing she had seen since Sigourney Weaver had killed off the bug from space?

Morgan turned around and gazed at Laura with a lazy smile. "Would you like something to drink?"

Laura was tired. And horny. And lost. And thirsty. *Drinking something can't hurt.* Surely Morgan wouldn't have rescued her just to poison her now. "Yes, please."

"I can only offer water." Morgan handed Laura an earthenware mug. "You must be thirsty after your little adventure tonight."

Laura snorted. *Little adventure. Very funny.* She took the mug and looked around for a place to sit down. There were neither chairs nor anything else that offered her a seat.

"I'm sorry." Morgan grimaced and rubbed her neck. "I don't have much company. There's only the bed to sit on."

"That's all right. I can stand."

"No. Please, sit down."

For a moment they looked into each other's eyes.

Morgan had two different colored eyes: one was green, the other brown, like the clothes she wore. Her eyes were gentle, and held a keen intelligence.

Laura coughed and looked away. *What is the matter with me? I don't know her and will probably never see her again.* She took a sip of water, enjoying the coolness of the liquid as it went down her throat. *This is really nice.* She stared into the mug. The water tasted of honey and cinnamon. Laura licked her lips and took another sip before asking, "What was all of that outside there? I'm still not sure if I'm dreaming…or if I'm drugged, or what the heck is going on."

There. She had said it.

Morgan tilted her head and studied Laura with an expression of disbelief, as if Laura was a child that didn't understand something she should. "It is Samhain. The veil between the worlds is thin tonight. Things that usually aren't allowed into this realm can exist here until the sun comes up again."

"But… You're joking, right?" Laura felt a pressure building in her chest. All of this couldn't be true. "This isn't real."

Morgan's brow furrowed. "Why wouldn't this be real?"

"Oh, I don't know. Maybe because all of this doesn't exist." Laura waved her hands around, indicating the cozy room. "I'm sure I'm dreaming…or something."

"No, you're not." Morgan crossed the distance between them and placed a soft kiss on Laura's lips.

Fiery tingles shot through Laura. Before she was able to process what was happening, the moment was over and Morgan had stepped away.

With an impudent grin on her face, Morgan asked, "Now— did that feel real, or not?"

"Are you mad?" Laura wiped at her mouth, breathing heavily. "Why did you do that?" *And why did you stop?*

"I have wanted to do that for a very long time." Morgan blew a strand of hair away from her face. "Are you tired?"

"What?" Laura was sure that her brain was about to explode at any moment. There was only so much that a girl could take.

"I asked whether you are tired. I am, and I would love to lie down. It was a surprise to see you tonight, a nice surprise, but I feel a bit drained."

Laura's gaze wandered to the bed. The not-so-big bed. The "two people can only sleep in there if they stay close to each other" kind of bed. The small devil on her left shoulder rubbed her hands and leered a "yes, nice"; the boring angel on the other shoulder shook her head and said "no way." Laura went with the boring angel's advice. "Nope. Not tired. Thank you."

Morgan laughed. "Are you afraid?"

"No." *Yes.* "Just not tired." Laura was afraid of her reaction to Morgan. She wanted too much to climb into bed and be kissed again and again…

Down, girl. She kissed you without asking your permission.

"But she's hot," a small voice in her head said. *"And she is just your type. Tall, strong, and a bit feisty."*

"Do you mind if I lie down?"

"No." Laura shook her head.

"Good." Morgan began to undo the buttons of her shirt.

"Oh. But…" Laura's breath stopped. A flash of heat raced

through her. *She can't—*

Morgan let the shirt fall to the floor.

Laura stared at Morgan's abdomen. A sun was tattooed around the navel in blue ink. The area around the sun was shining brightly and emitting light. Real light.

Morgan chuckled.

Heat rushed through Laura. She had been caught staring. Again. How embarrassing. Still…

Her gaze moved upwards, which was a terrible mistake. Morgan's breasts were white and round and inviting. Laura's fingers tingled with the urge to touch them. *Perfect. They are perfect.* She forced herself to stay still and balled her hands into fists. *This is crazy. I'm not that needy. But maybe this is just a dream…*

Morgan undid the buttons on her trousers and turned her back towards Laura.

Yes, I am that needy.

The most beautiful, lush tree Laura had ever seen dominated the strong back. Where the tattoo around Morgan's navel was done only in blue ink, the tree was bright and colorful, almost like a painting. No. It looked almost real. One could even imagine its crown moving in an imaginary wind. "Wow."

"Like what you see?"

"Can I touch it?"

Morgan gazed over her shoulder at Laura. "Yes. But once you touch it…touch me…I will want more."

Laura swallowed hard. What kind of night was this? And did she care any longer? Morgan was beautiful, perfect, but a stranger. And Laura still didn't know what was happening with her. On the other hand, for the first time in weeks, she felt desired. And she desired someone else in return. Heat simmered within her, a heat that she thought she had lost the capacity for since she had been betrayed. The thought of kissing Morgan again—and maybe investigating some other parts of her body, as well—made Laura's entire body stand to attention. She was more than willing to throw her qualms overboard…but she didn't. "I don't do one-night stands."

Morgan's laughter sounded like water running over well-worn stones. She tilted her head in question. "Why not? And who says it has to be?"

"I…" Laura didn't know what to say.

"It's perfectly safe."

"Is it?" Laura wanted Morgan. She wanted wild and crazy, and to be able to regret things in the morning.

"You can get to know me, again, if you want to." Morgan's voice was soft, inviting.

Again? Laura didn't understand, but she found that she didn't care. She squeezed her eyes shut. *I. Don't. Care. I want her. I want to lose myself. Just for one night.*

A featherlike touch on her cheek coaxed her to open her eyes and look straight into Morgan's: one blue, one brown. Gentle. Inviting.

"Come here." Morgan stretched out her hand.

Laura took it. The touch felt as cool as silk on her fevered skin. Goosebumps rippled across her body.

A small smile played around Morgan's eyes as she looked deeply into Laura's. "Let me undress you."

Unable to speak, Laura nodded. She stole a quick glance at Oz, who was already snoring away. "I'm a little nervous." The words were nothing but the plain truth. She was neither a player nor a very experienced lover.

Morgan's fingers cupped Laura's chin and drew her gaze up. "You don't need to be. You're the most beautiful woman I have ever seen."

There was sincerity in the gentle eyes. *She means it.* Discarding the last crumbs of her hesitation, Laura bent forward and kissed Morgan, teasing the soft lips until she was invited inside.

She couldn't remember how it happened, but it was only moments before they both were lying on the bed. Naked. Warm flesh on warm flesh.

Hot breath caressed the side of Laura's neck, setting shivers running through her body. Morgan bent down and took a nipple into her mouth. Laura groaned. Her whole body burned.

Soon full naked breasts were pressed against her. Running her hands over Morgan's back, Laura felt the supple muscles flex and twitch, soft flesh over muscles that were as hard as iron.

"Let me love you."

Morgan's voice cut through the fog in Laura's brain. When she realized that the warm body was gone, Laura opened her eyes. "No."

Morgan chuckled. From somewhere she had produced a small bottle. "This is oil. It smells like the sun on a wonderful summer day." Without further enquiry, strong fingers began to massage it into Laura legs.

Laura groaned with pleasure. This was heaven. She had imagined a quick fuck or a wild night. And hopefully that would follow later on. But to be touched like this, with reverence and near adoration... She couldn't remember when she had last felt that cherished. *A long, long time ago...if ever.*

A while later, there was not much of Laura's skin that had been left untouched. Laura was one quivering mass of boneless ecstasy and lust.

"You have wonderful skin, Laura. So soft, so lovely."

"Can I... I need to touch you as well."

A brilliant smile appeared on Morgan's face. "I'd love that." She put the bottle away.

Laura bent forward and covered Morgan's breasts. Hot, soft flesh filled her hands.

For long moments, no words were spoken. Only touch and sound existed.

Morgan dropped feather-light kisses down Laura's breasts, her belly, her hips, the tops of her thighs. She ran a finger along the rim of Laura's inner lips.

"Please." Pressure was building inside Laura. She needed to cum. Now.

"What do you want, Laura?"

"Stop teasing me."

"What do you want from life? What do you desire?"

Laura ground her teeth. Now Morgan wanted to talk?

"Tell me. The truth."

The truth? Laura didn't need to consider. Her defenses were down. "Life. To its fullest. To belong. But right now, I need you to touch me." Her voice sounded needy, even to her own ears.

"I will grant your wish, but only on my terms. Do you agree?"

Laura had no idea what Morgan was talking about. The only thing she knew was that she needed those strong fingers to finish what they had started. "Yes. Yes, I agree. Whatever."

"Good answer." Morgan's fingers returned to the needy spot, playing around Laura's clit. "I will fulfill your desire."

Laura's hands clutched the sheets when Morgan slid a finger inside, stroking sensitive spots in deliberate teasing.

At one point Laura felt a wetness around Morgan's fingers that seemed strange, but thought was soon replaced by a fluttering in her belly. Fire ripped through Laura, shooting lightning through her, wave after wave after wave, until her bones and muscles were nearly liquefied.

"Are you all right?" Morgan's voice was soft.

Laura snuggled up and enjoyed the sensation of being held in the strong arms. "Yes. If I was any more all right, I wouldn't exist."

Morgan chuckled. "We certainly don't want that." She brushed a light kiss on Laura's shoulder.

"That was the most intense orgasm I ever had." *And certainly never during a first time.* She took a deep breath. "I want to return the favor."

"There is no need—"

Laura's finger dipped into Morgan's wetness. "Oh, there is. A great need." She rubbed her finger over the warm, slippery flesh.

Morgan groaned.

Laura smiled. It would be a long night.

⍦

Laura opened her eyes. *A night of undisturbed sleep.* She smiled. Instead of a nightmare, she'd had the most erotic dream ever. She stretched, and the sheet slid over her body like the hands of the woman in her dream. *Wow! How can my muscles feel as if I really had sex for hours?*

Yawning, she sat up and swung her legs over the side of her bed. She wiggled her toes.

Oz lay in his basket, snoring, dead to the world.

Laura went into the bathroom and looked at herself in the mirror. Something about her face had changed. She looked younger. The bitterness around her mouth and in her eyes had vanished. Laura snorted. *If an erotic dream was all it took to get rid of that...* She wished she had dreamt one like that before. *Much better than another nightmare. And so real.*

She suddenly realized that she was looking at an empty spot around her neck. "Oh, shit." She had lost the necklace somewhere.

FOUR MONTHS LATER

"I'm sorry, Gail, but I'll be in late today. I seem to have picked up the stomach bug from hell." Laura pressed her hand against her stomach. She was really tired of throwing up every morning. "Could you please let Mr. Donaldson know that I will send his draft over tomorrow?"

"You should go and see your doctor." Her assistant's voice sounded concerned, even over the phone. "How long has this been going on?"

"For around a week."

"And you've been unusually cranky lately, plus, you didn't want any of the fabulous cheese Mr. Peters brought back for us. You love cheese. If you had a boyfriend, I would venture a guess that you're pregnant."

Laura chuckled. "Well, that would be the second immaculate conception in history. Thanks. I'll see you later, Gail."

Laura ended the call and took her cup of chamomile tea over to the sofa. Another morning of not being able to eat anything or even think about food without wanting to throw up. *Maybe Gail is right, and I should go and see a doctor.*

Like every other morning for the past couple of months, her eyes were drawn to the empty space on the sideboard where the photo of her and her ex had stood, before she had thrown it out.

The ringing of the doorbell echoed through the living room.

Oz barked twice before resettling on his favorite cushion and closing his eyes.

"You're my hero, Oz. Every thief is pissing his pants worrying about you."

Her only answer was a low growl.

Laura looked at her watch. Eight a.m. Strange time for a

visitor. With a sigh, she got up and went to the door. When she opened it, she found herself staring into her mother's brown eyes.

"Darling, I'm on my way to see Mildred, but I wanted to drop off something that arrived in the post for you a few days ago." She pressed a small, brown parcel into Laura's hand. "You should really let your friends know that you have your own place."

"They know, Mother."

"Well, obviously not everyone does." Her mother turned around and took the two steps down the front stairs to the street. "I have to hurry, dear." And with that, she vanished inside her Jaguar.

Laura shook her head as she watched her mother drive away. They hadn't spoken in two weeks. Once again, she was reminded that her mother wasn't interested in her life. No one really is. A wave of loneliness swept over her.

Who would send something for me to my parents' house?

She had moved out years ago. Her name and her parents' address were written in bold, beautiful handwriting. Laura looked for a return address on the parcel, but there was none. Neither was there a stamp, or any sign that the parcel had been delivered through the post.

She shook the parcel. Whatever was inside didn't make any sound. Well, at least it's not ticking, so it can't be a bomb.

With quick steps, she went into the kitchen, joined by Oz. She took a knife and carefully opened the small parcel. Inside was moss. Lush green moss.

Is this a joke?

How could the moss still be lush and green when the parcel had arrived days ago at her parents' place?

Maybe it is artificial moss. Laura picked up some of the green stuff. No, that is the real thing.

Something moved in the moss, and Laura let the bunch fall on the table. She took a step back, her eyes fixed on the greenery.

Nothing happened.

What was that?

She cautiously moved closer to the table.

There. Something did move.

Laura's heart beat faster.

Something small crawled out of the moss and stretched tiny arms and wings.

Laura took a deep breath. The air smelled of strawberries. That is…a Tinker Bell. Like in her dream. What—?

The butterfly-like Being took off and flew some circles around the table.

Oz barked like mad and ran around after it as if he wanted to catch the thing. Unfortunately, Boston Terriers didn't have wings.

Laura felt like she was having a heart attack. This can't be. This must be a dream. How—

The Being flew down until it was face to face with Laura.

Laura squinted at it.

The Being smiled and flitted even closer.

Laura took a few steps away from the table until her back was pressed against the wall.

The Being flew up to her, a smile on her tiny face. "She misses you." The voice was soft, and full of sunshine on a rainy day. It planted a kiss on Laura's cheek.

The Being flew to the window, pressed against the glass, and then re-appeared on the outside. With a wave, it disappeared.

"Shit." Laura's knees got weak, but she managed to get to a chair and plop down heavily. "Shit. Shit. Shit."

Oz sat down at her feet, panting like crazy.

"What was that?" Laura ran her hands through her hair. "I'm going crazy." She looked at the moss in front of her. Something brown caught her eye.

With trembling fingers, she fumbled for the brown bit and held it in her hand. Her pendant. The one she had lost in the cottage and hadn't been able to find. I can't believe this. Where did this come from?

She turned it around, and her breath caught in her throat.

This couldn't be her pendant. Instead of the two small stones that had been on the back, there were now three stones embedded in the wood. Two of them were a bit larger than the third one. With shaking fingers, she rubbed each of the three stones with her thumb.

A flash of lightning exploded before her eyes. Images of her dream lover flashed through her mind: Morgan in the throes of passion; orgasm after orgasm; Morgan's question, "What do you desire?" and Morgan's words "I will grant your wish, but only on my terms."

Morgan. Her dream lover. The only one Laura had had sex with in the past four months. But only in her dream.

Laura stared at the pendant. Oh shit!

Seconds later, she had the phone in her hand and was dialing her doctor.

The sonogram could just as well have been showing a tornado over England. This was simply not possible. She looked up into her doctor's eyes. "I can't be pregnant."

Her doctor's brow furrowed. "Well, you are. There are no two ways about it."

An hour later Laura stood outside her house, still shaking from the news. *Pregnant. This is impossible. Pregnant... Morgan...the pendant.* Round and round, her thoughts whirled.

Something clawed at Laura's memory. *Morgan...* Hadn't there been a Morgan...a long time ago?

Laura opened the door and rushed into her small office. With trembling fingers, she took one of her grandparents' old photo albums from the shelf. She had inherited those along with the cottage when her grandparents died.

She opened the album and began looking at the pages of photos. There she was, sitting under a tree, reading a book.

Another was of her playing with her grandmother's old Boston Terrier, Scarlett, in the garden at the cottage, throwing a ball for the dog to chase. And there was one of Laura swimming in the nearby lake. Laura with a girl a little older than herself, playing hide-and-seek between the trees. Laura and the same girl standing next to each other, both grinning like mad. Best friends. The little girl with the gap between her teeth... *What was her name?* Laura fought against the fog that enveloped her memories.

Morgan.

The girl's name had been Morgan. Like her dream lover.

I'm going mad.

Another memory catapulted to the forefront of Laura's mind.

Grandma's letter—

The last one Laura had received from her, it had arrived a week after her Grandmother's death.

Laura took the letter out of a box. There had been something in that letter, something she hadn't understood back then. She scanned the first three pages. There it was.

"Sweetheart. None of us can escape our Destiny, be it good or bad. Your Grandpa and I will not be with you much longer, but there is another that will always be looking out for you, watching over you. Your parents may not like this, may not even believe it, but some of us are meant to dance with the Faeries."

The letter shook in Laura's trembling fingers. On Shamhain, she had dreamt of Faeries and other supernatural creatures, of sex with Morgan. But had it really been a dream?

I'm pregnant.

"I know that one day you'll be ready to find your way, and your love, again. She will be here for you, waiting with the patience of a life that lasts nearly forever."

Laura's head hurt. Those words hadn't meant anything back

then, at least no more than words of consolation from a loving grandmother. But now…

Laura took another photo album off the shelf. This one was from the last summer she had spent with her grandparents. And there was the other girl again. Standing next to Laura, with her arm around her. Laura's gaze focused on something that was around the girl's neck.

The pendant.

Her grandmother's handwriting under the photo read "Meant to be—forever."

I will grant your wish, but only on my terms. Wasn't that what Morgan had said?

"Oh God, I'm pregnant! With a Faerie child!" Tears sprang into Laura's eyes. A storm was boiling inside her, her emotions tumbling uncontrollably.

She was pregnant. By Morgan.

Laura sat down heavily on the chair, her hand on her belly. *Pregnant. By a Faerie.*

She balled her fists in fury as she got up from her chair and stared down at Oz. "I'm going to hunt that damn Faerie down. And then we're going to have a long talk about joint custody and co-parenting!"

Oz whined.

"Sorry, boy. I'm not mad at you." She bent down and scratched him behind the ears.

Oz flopped onto his back and offered her his belly.

"Yes, you're the cutest pet," she rolled her eyes, "and the best mate ever."

Mate. She tasted the word. *Mate.*

What had the Butterfly Being said? "She misses you."

Laura's hand wandered to her belly. Something was growing inside her. No, not something—a child. Her child. *A huge responsibility.* A small smile crept on Laura's face. *And a wonderful gift.*

She went into the kitchen and picked up the pendant that was still lying on the table where she had left it earlier. She rubbed her thumb across the three embedded stones.

This time there were no memories or lightning flashing around in her head like a cheetah on dope. *Well, it seems to work only once.*

Still, it didn't take much effort to imagine Morgan's face. Her voice. Her hands, her beautiful hair—and her great ass.

She rescued me. The realization struck Laura for the first time. *And then she made love to me.* This hadn't all been about sex. *She even asked for my consent… in her own warped Faerie way.*

Laura walked over to the window and pressed her forehead against the cold glass. No butterflies were dancing around in the garden at this time of year. She wondered where the little Tinker Bell had disappeared to. *It's a long way to Ireland, to her sisters. I hope she's safe.*

It was a strange thing, but the concept of otherworldly beings didn't scare her any more…much. They were a reality that she had to accept. Her child would be half-Faerie.

One important question remained: What would a relationship with a Faerie like Morgan be like?

A grin spread across Laura's face. *Well, we'll see.*

♒

CHRYSALIS
by Joan Arling

1:32 AND THE EARTH WAS TEEMING with life, but the air above it was only sparsely populated by the fowl, so She created the aerial beings; small and mighty, She created them, the whisper and the storm.

The air was still, deadly quiet over the plain. The sun's light took on an eerie hue as silvery ice particles filtered through it in the upper layers of the atmosphere. Slowly, the winds that had brought the spicules descended from the stratosphere, sharply lowering the temperature of the warm humidity that had, until then, rested high above the ground, and when the water condensed, towering clouds appeared, only to be torn apart by blasts that would have caused an alteration in flight patterns, had the occurrence lasted long enough to be noticed by air control. The storm winds swirled down and down, causing ragged clouds to race through the lower levels of the atmosphere, and still the leaves hung motionless on the single tree standing in the middle of nowhere. Then, suddenly, the aerial phenomenon was over, the clouds dispersed, the ice dissolved, and the air returned to the quiet state it had exhibited before. The leaves on the solitary tree hung in the sunshine as if nothing had happened. The time had not yet come.

❧

Robert O'Hara wanted to light another cigarette, but thought better of it. Smoking was, of course, forbidden in the bleak, small room, but he would not have left it for anything. He resumed his pacing, six steps from the door through which he was denied passage and over to the window that looked out over the wind-swept clinic park, then six back from the window to the door he was denied...

"God, I can't stand this!"

The only other occupant of the small room turned to him. "You know, wearing away the carpet won't make things progress any faster. Your first?"

Robert winced at the words, at the same time thankful for the distraction. "Yes. Pretty obvious, isn't it?"

"Quite so."

"The damn—Excuse me, the nurse wouldn't let me in."

The sound of steps announced the nurse's approach. As she opened the door, the draught created between the leaky windows and the new opening increased the howling of the wind. She looked at Robert and smiled. "It's a girl—48 centimetres, 2800 grams. Both she and her mother are doing well. If you'd like..."

Her name was shortened to "Tara" before she even learned to walk. She acquired speech reasonably quickly, but early on she omitted the middle syllable of "Tamara," and before long, her parents adopted the shortened version.

Her mum and her dad watched her first steps as proudly as any parent has done since the beginning of history. However, Tara virtually skipped learning to walk, instead opting for learning to run. Run as fast as her legs would permit. If it took her longer than others to manage to stay upright, it was only because she was always, literally, a step ahead of herself. "Little Whirlwind," her father would say, a smug smile on his face.

The nickname was apt. Her parents soon took to setting moveable objects out of Tara's reach, as Tara seemed to find nothing amiss when things fell from a variety of surfaces, or travelled beautiful trajectories from her tiny hands to a wall or the floor, whichever they encountered first. By the age of two, the throwing of objects had stopped, but she still took little regard of things standing in her way, or of vases, dishes, or other breakables that had the bad fortune to be located near the edge of a table. Her father chalked the behaviour up to the boundless energy of the young, but her mother did not dismiss it as lightly, and she consulted a psychologist.

"She should go out more, you know, play with her friends. The presence of other children will help her assimilate, and I'm not talking about her succumbing to peer pressure or anything. It is absolutely normal for children to learn to conform to the group."

"Well...that is part of the problem. She does not, how can I put it, engage with other kids. Her friends are, to be frank, 'invisible.' When we ask her, she only says that she cannot pronounce their names."

"That is quite a common phenomenon. A lot of children have imaginary friends, often elves or fairies. It is probably a protection mechanism against the adult world, where most everything has to be accounted for. But it is rarely a matter for concern, only if it lasts well beyond the age of six or so."

"Look, Doctor, the other day she came running to tell me that she had seen the winds in the fields. The thing is, she spoke of them as if they were persons. When we went by a closed gate, she became very agitated, complaining that she was not able to pass that gate when all her 'sisters' could. She was obviously still talking about the 'winds.' Do you really think there is nothing to worry about?"

"Well...that is certainly interesting. But yes, I'd put it down to a very fertile imagination. Look at it as an early manifestation of creativity. Once channelled, she may well use the gift for creating works of art. Don't put her on too short a leash."

More assuaged than convinced, Violet O'Hara nevertheless decided to watch her daughter's behaviour rather than intervene. When Tara entered school, she became less outspoken about her "friends"—or "sisters," as she still occasionally referred to them—and she behaved much more normally, as judged by the yardstick of common sense standards. However...

"Tara, it's time for school. Are you coming down?"

Where are you? Why are you not here with us?'

Tara blinked her eyes. Never before had this...voice...been so intense. Awe-inspiring rather than intimidating, it seemed to draw nearer.

"Tara!"

"On my way, Mummy!"

"Tara! How many times do I have to tell you to close doors behind you?"

When she turned, she looked completely innocent. "But Mum, it's not fair to keep the winds out!"

"Look here, we've had to replace panes five times already. Do you think it is okay for your beloved winds to break the glass again and again?"

"But the winds don't care for barriers." Tara looked thoughtful. "If you didn't replace them, they could not be broken again."

Her mother rolled her eyes; she'd already been there too many times for her liking. Still, once more would probably not hurt.

"Windows keep out cold and rain. That is, as long as they're not broken. Would you rather have us freeze when the weather is bad?"

Tara was at a loss as to why her mother would ask a question that stupid, but she thought it wiser to keep her opinion to herself. "Me, I'd just lie in bed under my warm covers. Then the cold couldn't get at me."

"Tara, please, just close doors behind you, will you? Now come, school's waiting."

Violet O'Hara carefully closed the door behind her, thankful that Tara was occupied with skipping in the direction of the car.

⤸

All the classroom windows were open on that quiet

summer day. As usual, the attention the pupils their teacher left something to be desired; they would much rather have been playing outside. Tara had her gaze fixed on the horizon, when she noticed movement outside. Disregarding the admonishing looks from Mrs Mayberry, Tara went to a window and looked out at the single tree, whose branches were moving despite the still air. She waved, and suddenly a gust of wind filled the room, picking up papers from the desks and scattering them all about. Tara let out a cry of joy, clapping her hands in rapture while her mind was filled with wild laughter, and shouts of *'There you are!'* and *'My, you're a funny one.'* And amidst the chaos, that was only heightened by girls and teacher trying to get hold of the swirling papers, Tara stood without moving, filled with emotions for which she had no words.

Dear Mrs and Mr O'Hara,

As her teacher, I write on behalf of Tamara. I must admit that I am quite concerned about her behaviour. She is obviously a very intelligent child, as all the tests certify, yet she often seems to be disconnected from reality. It is not that all unusual for girls to have 'invisible friends,' or act in other ways that tend to disquiet adults, but in my experience, Tara should be past that stage by now.

Tamara has some very firm conceptions that seemingly cannot be shaken, even in the face of facts. Above all, she believes that wind is not a natural phenomenon, but that 'the winds' are persons with distinct personalities. She listens to them, maintaining that they tell her stories, even calling her to become one of them. When in such a state, she is unable to follow the lessons, and is virtually unapproachable by either me or her classmates. I do sincerely hope that this is just a passing stage in her development, but I am uneasy enough about her current behaviours that I want to most respectfully suggest you take her to a psychologist to gain more insight. Just to be on the safe side.

Yours sincerely,
Helen Mayberry

᷎

The weather forecast had been anything but encouraging. A tempest was brewing, and everybody was urged to stay inside, close doors and windows, and bolt the shutters, if available.

Towering clouds began to thicken, until they looked virtually black from below. The wind picked up force and soon reached storm velocity, showing no signs of relenting. And then it began to rain. The torrents from the sky, that swamped the earth in minutes, were soon joined by hail. Pieces of ice as thick as a thumb were driven almost horizontally against the wall, producing a sound like a mad drummer in the midst of his life's solo.

There was a sudden crash as the window of Tara's room was hurled open, breaking the panes. Her parents ran upstairs, flung open the door to her room, and were transfixed by the sight that met their eyes: Her clothes drenched, Tara stood in front of the broken window, bleeding from several cuts caused by the flying shards. Her eyes were closed and her arms were open, and she seemed oblivious to the presence of the adults.

'Come! Come with us!'

'How? And where?'

'Come fly with us, fast, free!'

'I can't. Not yet!'

Within minutes, the wind settled, the sky cleared, and the afternoon sun heated the wetness into clouds of vapour even while there was still hail glistening on the ground.

Tara opened her eyes and turned around. "Hi Mum, Dad. My friends came to see me, but they're gone already..." She looked at the glass lying on the ground. "Oh. Don't be mad at them, please? They were so excited to see where I live."

"I don't expect to ever understand this, but can we be at least clear on one point? Friends, sisters, or what?"

Tara looked at her mother with puzzlement. "What's the difference?"

"And why do you only call them sisters? No brothers?"

Tara shook her head. "There couldn't be," she stated with conviction.

"And why not?"

Mothers could ask funny questions. "Because I don't like boys."

∾

"TARA! Come down AT ONCE!"

Tara stood on the roof of the stable, a little uncertain of her footing but her gaze steadily fixed on the horizon. When her mother's voice registered, she looked down the considerable distance, and wondered what the intensity was about. "But Mummy, I can see so far from up here. And I believe I can fly!"

"NOOO!"

But Tara was already running, her little arms stretched out in imitation of the birds' wings she had seen the wind carry. When she reached the edge, she jumped, and hit the ground with a thud that made her mother's heart stop.

She awoke in a white room that made her uneasy, and looked about her, even though moving her head made her feel disoriented. "Mum?"

"Oh, little one...you're back. Thank God!" Violet O'Hara almost levitated from the seat she had been occupying all of the day and most of the night before, and hurried over to the bed. "I've been so worried. Are you in pain? Can I get you anything, like French fries, or something? I'm certain I would have to smuggle it past the nurses, but... " Her voice faltered.

"No, Mummy, I feel alright. A little dizzy, perhaps. My arms and my legs hurt, though." Her face took on a forlorn expression. "I was so certain I could do it."

"Fly? Oh, my precious! Flying is what birds do. Please never ever try to do this again! I almost died when I saw you hit the ground. You could have been killed!"

"But I will learn, Mum." She yawned. "I'm so tired." And with that, she fell asleep.

∾

Tara wondered what the therapist wanted to hear from her. Her only wish was to go where the winds went, and her only problem was that she couldn't. *Yet*, she thought. She doubted that the therapist would be able to do anything about that.

"What do they tell me? They talk about the refreshing feeling of rising very high, where they get cooled down and thinned out at the same time. About how they drink in the vapours out over the sea, and how different that tastes compared to the mists from a lake. How the sun sometimes heats them up so much that they just have to run in order to expend the energy. Sometimes they meet to dance together, and when they are many, they love to form interlocking spirals. When they're really into a fling, lots of tiny things fly around like they want to participate. They laugh a lot about that."

The therapist blanched at the innocent description of a—what, hurricane, cyclone? She was no meteorologist, but she'd seen the satellite pictures in the news.

"And when they tell you their stories, how do you feel about it?"

"It makes me happy for them, and at the same time I am sad that I cannot go with them. I belong with them, and they know it. That's why they come see me time and again. They are waiting for me to get ready."

A hushed whisper, full of expectation, barely stirred the air. 'Is this the time? We've waited for so long!'

Tara got out of bed with the strange feeling that her body only followed her soul unwillingly, kind of lagging behind. She tried to ignore the slight disorientation, slowly navigating the stairs, then taking careful aim at the door, making certain that she had a firm grip on the handle before opening it. Once she was out of the house, progressing became easier. She walked through grass wet with early morning dew, and sat down with her back against the tree, closed her eyes, and let the air caress her skin.

'We're here for you. Now's the time! Come, come join us.'

It felt like drifting off into slumber, and when, at last, she lost the connection, it was only like the slightest of tugs. Dislodging some of the leaves on her way, she rushed straight up, and moved in dancing circles, which were soon matched by those of her sisters. She dived down again and circled the tree, against which leaned the body of a girl, apparently in a deep, dreamless sleep.

'Do you think you'll have any more need for this?'

She swirled around the tree once more, trying to remember something that seemed to connect her to the still figure. Then, rejoicing in the welcome from her many sisters, Tara swung herself up and joined them in their race towards the horizon, not looking back once.

♒

SISTERS OF THE MOON
by Diane Marina

THUNDER BOOMED OVERHEAD and wind rattled the windows of Nicole's Fiat as she battled after-work traffic on a late October Thursday night. The romantic in her loved an occasional rainy day, but the sky had bled rain for four of the past six days, and that had given a gloomy overtone to the entire week.

This is becoming ridiculous, she thought, as she maneuvered around the car of a fellow commuter. Her mood soured, she pounded the steering wheel in frustration. "That's it," she said aloud to herself. "When I get home, I'm packing and moving to California. This Maryland weather is for the ducks."

Nicole jumped as music blared from her backpack. "I'm Sexy and I Know It" ring tones could signify just one person: Danni. Nicole was tempted to answer the call from her best friend, but was not about to get ticketed for talking on her cellphone while driving.

The wipers slapped across the windshield, and Nicole moved her face closer to better see where she was going. *Thank goodness traffic is crawling, or I might drive off the road in this God-awful weather.* The cell buzzed, indicating that Danni had left a message. For a second Nicole considered listening, but then the Fiat hit standing water, demanding her full attention. She scowled, wiping the condensation on the window while traffic crawled.

Thankful that her waterfront apartment was only three miles from the medical center where she worked as a nurse, Nicole pulled her compact car into her assigned space in the lot. Her head dropped back against the headrest in relief. After a moment, she pushed the driver's door open against the elements and scurried out before the wind could slam the door against her.

Nicole stepped from the car straight into a puddle. "Erghh." A quick glance at the parking lot told her the entire area resembled a wading pool. Groaning, she pushed her drenched hair from her face, grabbed her backpack and empty coffee mug, and bumped the door closed with her hip. The shoe that had landed in the puddle squished as she trudged across the parking lot to her apartment complex.

Inside the lobby of her apartment building, Nicole shook off the rain while she waited for the elevator. Despite the bleak mood trying to settle over her, Nicole smiled when she realized she probably looked like her dog Tater after one of their evening walks in the rain. It felt good to be home and out of the storm.

The sound of her key in the lock prompted some deep woofs from the other side of the door, along with the skittering of claws as Tater scampered to the door to greet her. Nicole dropped her belongings in the entryway and scooped the hound into a hug.

"Okay, Sparky," Nicole greeted, using one of tens of nicknames she'd created for her dog. "Let Mommy get changed, and we'll get some Kibble in you and then get you outside to do your stuff." She was amused by how quickly just a few doggie kisses could lift her mood and make her willing to step back out into the rain and muck. "But let me give Aunt Danni a call first to see what she wants."

Nicole poured some dry food into the dog's dish and then fished her phone from her bag. Not bothering to listen to her voicemail, she pushed wet hair from her face and hit the "call back" button. Her best friend answered on the second ring.

"Nicks! How's it goin', babe?"

Danni was crunching on something that should not be eaten while on the phone.

"You called me first. What's up with you? And put down those kettle chips." Nicole laughed into the phone. She knew Danni's habits all too well. She looked like a supermodel, but ate, drank, and swore like a sailor. If Nicole were a betting person, she'd have wagered that Danni would soon be belching. Improving her odds, she heard Danni take a swig from a bottle.

"Dude, I'm starving. No time for lunch today. What a brutal day. Anyway, I got us tickets for tomorrow night. Pick me up at six in your little roller skate." Nicole heard more crunching and then a muffled "Steph's going with us too."

Nicole rubbed her forehead. *There go my plans for a quiet weekend.* "Danni," she began, as if talking to a three-year-old, "slow down and explain to me why I'm picking you up and where we're going. I don't have anything on my calendar." After a short moment of silence, she heard a small hiccup on Danni's end.

"Boo Crawl!" Danni squawked.

Nicole briefly considered whether her friend was speaking in tongues or her words were being garbled by her snacking. "Danni, what the—"

"Boo Crawl, Nicks! Did you *not* listen to my voicemail? You didn't, did you?" Danni scolded.

Nicole shook her head, but before she could say anything, Danni continued.

"Annapolis is having a pub crawl and ghost tour, now through Halloween. I got us tix, babe! We'll get to hit a few bars and hear all the ghoulishly grisly details of all of the haunted joints downtown. Righteous, right?

Crunch, crunch.

"And I invited Steph to go as my date. I figure the beer will loosen her up, and the stories about things that go bump in the night will scare her right into my arms. Heh, heh."

Nicole knew that Danni was all bark and no bite. *Poor Steph. I hope she gets Danni's humor.*

Her shoulders slumped. She had been looking forward to a quiet weekend to herself. "Tomorrow night? That doesn't give me much lead time. Is the rain even supposed to stop by then?" Nicole groaned as Tater finished her dinner and began dancing around, obviously ready for the next step in their nightly routine.

"Not sure, but who cares?" Danni responded, oblivious to Nicole's mood. "A little rain will add to the spooky factor. Live a little, bud. Maybe we'll find you a chick to snuzzle up against before the night is over. Just bring your beer goggles." Danni guffawed.

Nicole leaned against the kitchen doorframe. Her week at work had been long and arduous, and her plans for the weekend had included nothing more strenuous than reading a good book and cleaning her bedroom. She knew Danni would not take no for an answer and would rib her for being what she called a spinster before her time. "Danni—"

"See you at six. Wear comfy shoes, but not too comfy. Hot chicks don't like girls who dress like librarians. Or like nurses, for that matter, so change before you pick us up," she instructed. She tossed in a "love ya" before ending the call.

Maybe Danni is right. A night out could be just what I need. Nicole shrugged and placed her phone on the kitchen counter, then removed Tater's leash from a nearby hook. "Okay, butter bean, let's get this over with. Our time together this weekend is suddenly limited. Let's make the most of today."

Nicole huddled together with Danni and Steph in front of one of the shops in the Annapolis historic district. The rain had stopped, but a gauzy fog hung over the streets. Fat puddles left over from the previous day's rain dotted the sidewalks, and cautious pedestrians had to watch their step.

Nicole threw her head back and gazed upwards. The sky was somewhat clear despite the light fog, and the moonlight created an eerie glow. She closed her eyes and hoped that this was an omen that Mother Nature might show some mercy. She listened peripherally to the flirting between Steph and Danni, while hordes of weekend revelers strolled by. Many were from the nearby Naval Academy, some still in their smart uniforms, but all were out for a night of fun from the looks of it. She glanced down at Annapolis Harbor, at the small private boats bobbing on the waves that rolled into the inlet. She loved this city, especially at night, when the streets came alive.

A man approached them carrying a lantern and dressed as a revolutionary town crier. "You ladies here for the ghost tour and pub crawl?" When they nodded, he said, "Have you got your tickets?"

Danni reached into the inner pocket of her jacket and yanked out three tickets. "Yep, got 'em right here, buddy. Are you going to scare our socks off tonight, or will we get too drunk to notice?" She laughed loudly.

Steph, who seemed quite lovestruck already, giggled at Danni's attempt at humor.

"It's a good tour. You'll have the chance to learn some of the history of Annapolis, as well as try some local brews. As long as you don't overindulge *too* much, you should have a great time. We'll get started in a few minutes. I see some others that I have to wrangle. My name's Troy, by the way. Hold on to your tickets, and I'll be back in a bit."

Danni and Steph continued their shenanigans beside her, and Nicole scrunched her nose and crossed her arms. *I should have stayed home. I never feel like a third wheel when I'm home with Tater.*

Troy returned and motioned for them all to gather around so that he could collect their tickets. Within minutes, the tour began with a group that was relatively small — fewer than a dozen people—which allowed their guide to interact with everyone in the group as they ambled through town.

The others on the tour seemed eager for a night of fun. There was chatting and laughter between stops, and Nicole joined in, warming to the enthusiasm of the group. She noted with a grin that Steph was either genuinely unnerved by the stories, or the spooky nuances of the evening were her excuse to find shelter in Danni's protective embrace.

Troy drew the group in around him at each predetermined site, his lantern held high for dramatic effect as he shared the gruesome history of each stop. Nicole was wide-eyed as she listened, intrigued by the history in the tales.

As the group stopped in front of a small stone house, not far from the town center, a breeze kicked up and Nicole shivered. When Troy turned toward the group and stood stock still, the crowd grew quiet.

"Do you all see this house behind me?" he asked.

There were murmured responses and a few nervous giggles.

"This house is the most haunted house in Annapolis, perhaps even in the state of Maryland."

The people on the tour were silent; the only sound in the area was a distant whoosh as a car drove down a wet adjacent street.

Nicole's skeptical mind began a tour of its own. *How do these guys know these things? Do they go door to door grilling each homeowner? Like a census worker for the Undead. Excuse me, could you tell me how many living residents you have here? How about Undead?*

When she realized that she had been giggling over her own mental meanderings, Nicole's attention snapped back to Troy's narrative, but she caught Danni watching her.

Danni shrugged and mouthed, "What are you doing?"

Nicole's face flushed with embarrassment, and she waved her hand dismissively.

Troy was continuing in a sinister tone. "The last family fled, leaving most of their belongings behind. You probably noticed that a few of the rooms have a light on, including the one behind me."

Several in the crowd nodded.

"If you look closely into this living room window, you'll see there are motion detector cameras around the entire room. They're in almost every room of the house, and when movement is detected, these lights go on." Troy stopped for effect. "Did I mention that you can see the detector in the living room because the light is on?"

A cold chill crept up Nicole's spine. She wrapped her arms around herself and moved closer to Danni and Steph.

"Okay, let's move on." Troy moved forward with a pleased grin.

As they walked back toward the center of town to the first pub stop, Danni slowed her pace to wait for Nicole. "Pretty creepy, huh, bud? Or in your case, pretty funny. What was that grinning all about back there?"

Nicole managed a weak smile. "Nothing. Just punchy, I guess." When the other tour-goers stopped at Troy's direction, she looked up and chuckled. "The Rusty Rudder Tavern? Wow. They couldn't have come up with a better name than that?" The laughter bubbled up again. *I must be more tired than I realized.*

Danni joined her in laughter. "Are you having a good time?"

"Yes, I am," Nicole replied. "You two seem to be getting along. Very well." She nodded toward Steph.

Danni chuckled and shoved her hands into the pockets of her leather bomber jacket. "Yeahhh. I hope we get along even better later on." With another laugh, she nudged Nicole with her elbow and stepped up her pace to re-join her date.

A flare of jealousy tugged at Nicole as she watched them. She would be the first to admit that it had been too long since she'd been in a relationship, and cuddling up to the dog didn't quite fill the void. Nicole shook her head and exhaled forcefully, determined to rid herself of the sudden melancholy which she attributed to the persistently bad weather. She strode toward Danni and Steph, and linked her arm through Danni's free one.

Danni looked surprised at first, but then beamed as she nodded toward the entrance of the pub. "Let's go get some brews, ladies!"

They stepped into the tavern, straight into a sweltering room packed with weekend revelers. Nicole could barely hear herself over the noise when she turned toward Danni to say, "I'm going to run to the ladies room. Can you get me something light, like a Pilsner?" Nicole reached into the pocket of her jeans for some cash.

Danni placed her hand on Nicole's shoulder. "On me, no worries."

Nicole nodded her thanks and squeezed toward the back of the crowded pub, where she hoped to find the restroom. As she walked down the stone-walled hallway, she noted that the building looked ancient. The scent of the aged, uneven wood floor tickled her nose. The rich smell reminded her of the first day of school, and the essence of the old floors that had been varnished during the summer break. *Definitely an old building.*

She wanted to hurry back to hear the history of the bar, and was relieved to see that there was no line for the restroom. A woman stood at the row of sinks, her back to the door. Nicole could see her face in the mirror and was transfixed by her beauty. Jet black hair fell in waves past the woman's shoulders, and long lashes shrouded her eyes until she looked up and smiled at Nicole in the mirror. She gazed at Nicole as if she was very pleased to see her. Goosebumps broke out on Nicole's skin as the woman's icy blue eyes locked onto hers, and a flutter stirred in Nicole's belly.

Nicole returned the smile and then bit her lip, trying to tamp down the butterflies she was feeling. *Is she flirting with me?* The tingling along her skin grew in intensity. Nicole proceeded into the nearest stall, hoping the woman would be still be there when she came out.

She was. Her hip resting against the counter, her arms folded, her smile still present.

The woman seemed dressed for Halloween. *An employee?*

"Hello," the woman greeted.

Nicole moved to the sink to wash her hands. The chills disappeared and were replaced by a warm flush at the sound of the woman's voice. The low, whiskey-soaked timbre made Nicole's spine tingle in such a pleasant way.

"Hi," Nicole barely puffed out, her sudden nervousness apparent in her voice. Heat started in her chest and climbed her neck, finally settling in her cheeks.

"I didn't see you here earlier. I know the bar is crowded, but I would have remembered you." The woman smirked, and she tapped her fingers along her arm as she watched Nicole.

There was something so familiar about the woman. Perhaps

her charm and self-confidence reminded Nicole of Danni's cockiness with women. She oozed sexiness, in the way she watched Nicole, and in the way she smiled with just one side of her mouth upturned. Despite the attraction she was feeling, Nicole had every intention of resisting any flirtation. The woman was just too sure of herself; Nicole was determined not to succumb to her advances. Despite her resolution, Nicole's eyes fell on the woman's generous breasts, which filled her lacy blouse and peaked over the top of her low cut bodice.

The woman's smile grew. "I'm Liz." She extended a fine, porcelain hand. "Tell me you have a name as beautiful as you are."

The heat in Nicole's face blazed. "I'm uhhh, Nicole." *Idiot!* She raised a hand to her cheek, hoping to hide the bright flush.

"Mmmm, a beautiful name indeed." Liz spoke as if she hadn't noticed Nicole's discomfort. "I work here at the pub." Her gaze slowly lapped over Nicole's body. "I hope you'll let me buy you a drink."

"Thank you, but my friends are buying me one as we speak. I'm here with a ghost tour, and..."

Liz had moved closer with each word Nicole spoke, and now she placed a hand on Nicole's waist. Without warning, she kissed her soundly on the mouth.

An electric bolt of desire stabbed at Nicole's belly before warning bells sounded the need for caution. "Wha...what was that about?" Nicole placed a hand against Liz's shoulder and pushed her away. Her breaths came in shallow gasps; her fists balled in anger at her sides. The fury rose within her, and she had to stop herself from slapping Liz. *Bar wench...her uniform is pretty appropriate, considering her behavior!*

Liz regained her composure and moved closer again. Placing her hand on Nicole's hip, she said, "I'm sorry, I... It's just that...well, I thought I read interest in your eyes." Liz's gaze trailed to Nicole's mouth.

"Stop that!" Nicole pushed Liz away again and stormed past her. "I have half a mind to talk to your manager!" Nicole turned and barreled through the swinging door.

She rushed into the main pub room and found Danni and Steph in a corner near the door. She barely saw them through the anger that propelled her. The tour guide appeared to be finishing up a story, gesturing at the bar behind him.

"Hey, Nicks." Danni held out a beer. "We thought you fell in." She swigged her beer and nodded at Troy. "You missed a great story!"

Nicole accepted the beer and took a healthy chug. The cold drink felt soothing on her hot throat. Her brow furrowed, and she swiped at a coating of sweat on her forehead. Her mind replayed the bathroom incident again and again. She was shaking with anger at the woman's arrogance and presumption, but, admittedly, also from excitement. Despite Liz's brash behavior, Nicole had found her attractive and the kiss had thrilled her. She could still feel the heat of Liz's lips.

"Everything okay, bud?" Danni was watching her with a frown. "You seem shaken."

Nicole nodded and took another generous sip of her beer. "I'm fine. There was a woman in the bathroom, and she got a little pushy. She…she tried to kiss me. She *did* kiss me." Even to herself, Nicole thought her voice sounded breathy, and she hoped Danni hadn't noticed. She didn't want to be asked questions she didn't have answers to.

Danni grinned. "Whoa, what? Was she cute?"

Nicole dipped her chin and her brow crinkled. "Danni, I'm serious! Don't joke."

"Sorry, Nicks. Who is she? Do you want me to go talk to her?"

Nicole hung her head. "No. No, just let it go. I'm not even sure exactly what happened. It all happened so quickly, and I guess… Well, I guess I may have sent mixed signals. She was certainly attractive."

Her eyes skimmed the bar to see if Liz had returned to work. "Just forget it. Tell me what I missed." Her eyes moved from patron to patron as she drank her brew, but there was no sign of Liz.

Danni pulled Steph closer and slung an arm around her

shoulder. She had to talk loudly to be heard over the din of noisy patrons. "You missed a good tale. A murder took place here a long time ago. Spooky stuff!"

Troy announced that the tour would be leaving for the next pub within minutes, and encouraged the trio to finish their beers. He downed his own drink and moved on to alert the others.

"I'd better hit the bathroom before we move on," Danni said. "Sure you don't want me to take care of business if I run into that babe?"

"No. Just forget I said anything. I'm fine." *I think.*

Danni and Steph disappeared into the crowd, and Nicole took the opportunity to move up to the bar and set down her empty glass. She had turned to go outside when she caught sight of Liz, who was standing at the far end of the main room, watching her with a pensive look. Liz grinned in a way that appeared apologetic, and Nicole moved toward her. Nicole hesitated, debating whether or not to give Liz another chance. *Go on, stop being so stubborn!*

"Can I get you another, hon?" someone asked from behind the bar.

Nicole glanced over at Liz and then shook her head at the bartender.

"Let's go, bud!" Danni said as she cruised past, Steph in tow.

Hesitating, Nicole turned back to where Liz stood. She was gone.

∽

Later that evening, Nicole was settled into bed with Tater, who was sound asleep at her side. A magazine lay on her lap, open but unread as she played with Tater's fur. She leaned against the pillows and rested her head against the headboard as she thought about the evening. She felt a little numb from the few drinks she'd had, but she was nowhere near inebriated. Knowing that she had to drive her friends and herself home, she had sipped from a bottle of water during the last few stops. Danni and Steph, on the other hand, had been considerably over the legal limit and were probably a drunken mass of tangled limbs by now. She smirked as she thought of her friend getting her wish for the evening.

"Hey, Tater, I bet your Aunt Danni got lucky tonight." She patted the sleeping dog's head. "That makes one of us. God, I'm pathetic."

Nicole closed her eyes and allowed her mind to wander over the rest of the evening. Recalling the kiss, she pressed her fingers to her lips. Liz was most definitely a beautiful woman. Nicole was drawn to her, and if she were being brutally honest with herself, she had to admit that she liked Liz's aggressive behavior. Unaccustomed to having women act in such a forward manner, she'd pushed her away, but the attraction Liz had sensed in Nicole had been present.

She blew out a breath and closed her magazine, then tossed it on the bedside table. "Tater, I guess Mama's just going to have to go back there and give her another chance...if she's still interested, that is."

Tater didn't stir from her slumber as Nicole kissed the top of her head and turned off the lamp before settling down to sleep.

Nicole sat behind the wheel of her car and checked her reflection in the rearview mirror for the umpteenth time. "Drat!" She sat back and dropped her head against the headrest before leaning forward and looking in the mirror yet again. "Why don't they make these mirrors face-sized?"

The evening following the ghost tour, Nicole had driven to the pub directly from work, and now she was regretting that she hadn't gone home first to change and add some makeup. She wore her scrubs, now grimy from a full day's work at the hospital, and her hair was limp from running up and down hallways all day.

"Maybe this was a bad idea."

She groaned as she leaned back and considered her options. She could go home, shower, change, and come back. But by that time, she'd be ready to go to bed and wouldn't want to venture out. She could go into the pub and make the best of the situation, hoping Liz wouldn't notice her less-than-glamorous state. Or she could sit here in the vehicle all night, thinking about what might be.

She banged her head on the steering wheel with a small thud. Gathering up the courage she hadn't been sure she had, she opened the door and stepped out of the car and headed toward the pub.

"You'll be fine." Step. Step.

"She's just a girl." Step. Step.

"She's a very *hot* girl." Step, Step.

"She's a very hot girl who *kissed* you. Holy crap."

Nicole stopped and gaped at the entrance. "Okay, it's now or never. I hope she likes women who talk to themselves in public."

She gazed up at the moonlit sky and felt as if the glow was nudging her toward the door. A sharp wind whipped around her and sent a shiver up her spine. She wrapped her leather jacket tightly around herself and opened the door to the pub. The clink of glasses and murmur of the crowd washed over her. She licked her lips and glanced around, dodging a server carrying an overhead tray just in time.

Raking her hand through her hair, Nicole looked around to get her bearings. She moved toward the bar and ordered a ginger ale, tapping her nails on the bar while she waited for her drink. She chewed the inside of her cheek and frowned. Where was Liz? The bartender brought Nicole's drink, and she tossed a couple of bills on the bar.

Nicole turned her head, and her gaze was captured by a white flowing sleeve disappearing in a nearby doorway—the same doorway where she'd seen Liz standing, watching her, the night before. She took her soda and moved in that direction. Liz was leaning in the doorway, smiling, arms crossed. Nicole's heart raced as she moved closer.

Liz gazed at Nicole through her thick lashes. "I hoped you would come back."

Nicole was barely able to hear Liz's voice over the din of the crowd.

"I...well, truthfully, I haven't been able to stop thinking about you." Nicole's cheeks grew hot, and she took a gulp of her soft drink.

Liz's smile just touched the corners of her mouth. "Good, I'm glad. Come with me to a quiet spot where we can talk." Liz took Nicole's glass and set it on a nearby tray. "I'll get you another one later, if you'd like." She extended her hand to Nicole.

Nicole hesitated. *This is crazy. What am I doing here? I don't even know this woman!*

Liz extended her hand further.

What the hell. I've got nothing to lose. Nicole placed her hand in Liz's and followed her through a narrow hallway to a door marked "EXIT." The chill of the night air hit Nicole, and she wrapped her arms around herself against the cold.

Her smile radiant, Liz leaned against the building and studied Nicole. "I'm glad you came back. I was afraid I had scared you away."

Nicole shivered and fussed with her hair. She looked at Liz's dress, the same as she had worn the night before, and wondered how she managed to keep from freezing in the chill night air.

Liz held Nicole's restless hands. "Are you nervous?"

Nicole looked into Liz's eyes. Their color today appeared to be a muted blue, almost as if they were shrouded in a fog. Nicole looked closer and Liz blinked, breaking the spell.

"Yes, I guess I am a little nervous." She moved closer to Liz, and noticed a spicy cologne that she hadn't been aware of before. The scent reminded Nicole of cardamom and cinnamon, with just a hint of pleasant musk thrown in. It was intoxicating. "I apologize for my reaction last night. You took me by surprise when you...well, when you..."

"When I kissed you?"

Nicole nodded.

"Like this?" Liz moved closer to Nicole, her gaze fixed on Nicole's lips.

Their lips met, and Nicole did not resist. She kissed Liz without inhibition, parting her lips to allow Liz's tongue to dip inside. Nicole moaned at the contact and deepened the kiss.

Liz slid her hands under Nicole's jacket and scrub top, her thumb making lazy circles along the flesh of her rib cage.

Nicole moaned again as goosebumps rose on her skin. Liz's lips were mesmerizing, and Nicole didn't want to stop kissing her. Nicole whimpered when Liz tore her mouth away and moved her lips to Nicole's neck, nibbling from her ear to her collarbone, leaving warmth and wetness in their wake.

"You're driving me crazy. What time do you get off work?" Nicole asked in short puffs of breath.

Liz chuckled into Nicole's hair. "I am *always* working, I'm afraid. Let's just enjoy each other right here and right now." Liz gazed into Nicole's eyes.

Nicole squinted and tilted her head back a bit to better see Liz, whose eyes now seemed a radiant blue. Liz kissed her again, and Nicole was lost in the caress of Liz's velvet mouth.

"I could kiss you forever," Liz whispered into Nicole's mouth.

Nicole sighed and pressed her lips against Liz's.

Liz pulled away with a slight huff. "But I'm afraid I have to get back to work. Thirsty people become angry people." She laughed.

Nicole wanted to protest, but she loved her job and would have made the same decision had the roles been reversed. She frowned, but nodded her understanding. "I don't want you to lose your job. Can I see you again?"

Liz's smile was electric. "Of course you can. I would love to see you again. Can you come by on Tuesday night? We'll be much less busy then, and I'll have time to spend with you. It's the night before Halloween, so we should have a small crowd if any."

Nicole responded with a smile of her own. "Absolutely. I'll come right after work again."

Liz kissed her again, melting Nicole's insides with the sweetness of the kiss.

Liz gently pushed Nicole away from her. "Well, Nicole, I do have to get back to work, but I am very much looking forward to Tuesday evening. Let me walk you back to the bar."

After a quick peck on the lips, Liz turned and opened the door, allowing Nicole to walk ahead of her into the establishment. When they neared the front door, Nicole turned and hugged Liz.

Liz kissed her cheek and whispered, "See you Tuesday." Without another word, she turned and disappeared through the doorway where Nicole had spotted her earlier that evening.

Nicole couldn't help smiling as she left the bar and walked toward her car with nothing on her mind but seeing Liz again on Tuesday night.

❦

Nicole hurried down the hospital corridor carrying an IV bag, her cellphone propped between her head and shoulder and pressed against her ear. She navigated around the gurneys parked in the corridor as she tried to focus on what Danni was saying.

"Danni, I can't just leave work. It doesn't matter that my shift is over, we've had an emergency and the hospital needs all available staff." She shook her head as she dropped the IV bag on the countertop at the nurses' station. On the other end of the line, Danni was enumerating the reasons she thought Nicole should leave work.

I should have just called Liz myself. It would have taken less time than this conversation.

Nicole chewed on her thumbnail. *If I hang up now, I wonder if I can just put in a quick call and leave a message for Liz.*

As her frustration with Danni grew, Nicole slapped her forehead with her palm. "Do you *not* understand what I'm saying? People have died in this pileup, and we have half a dozen casualties here, some of whom might not make it. I'm needed here, Danni."

Danni sighed. "Okay, Nicks. Just tell me what you want me to do."

Nicole puffed out the breath she'd been holding. *Thank God.* "I need you to either call the Rusty Rudder Tavern or stop in and explain to Liz that I can't make it tonight, but tell her that the only reason I didn't come is because of a life or death situation. Please do that for me. Oh, and ask her when she's working again, so I can stop in to see her."

"Yeah, yeah, sure I will, bud. I don't want your promising love life imploding before it has a chance to take off."

"Thank you." Nicole stopped in the hallway. She needed to get off the phone so she could deliver a saline IV. "Please tell her I'm sorry, and I'll stop in as soon as I can." Without waiting for a reply, Nicole snapped her phone shut and pocketed it, and then dashed into a nearby hospital room.

Two days later, Nicole was driving her Fiat through the dark streets of Annapolis. It was the night after Halloween, and the empty streets seemed to be mourning the loss of holiday revelers. The rain had started up again, and the only thing that kept Nicole from feeling sullen was that she was driving to the tavern to see Liz. She had been disappointed to hear that Danni had called the tavern, and had been told by the woman who answered the phone that she would try to find someone named Liz to give her Nicole's message.

The multi-car accident had resulted in many additional patients being brought in. Nicole was relieved that no additional lives were lost and those who were seriously injured were recovering or stable, but she had had no time off for two days.

Nicole was glad she had no trouble finding a parking space near the tavern. She didn't have an umbrella, and the rain continued at a steady pace. It was bad enough she had to again come directly from work and dressed in her soiled scrubs, she didn't want to look like a drowned rat, too. She checked herself in the rearview mirror, shrugged, and exited the car, then jogged toward the tavern in order to minimize the effects of the rain.

Inside the tavern, she fluffed her hair. The atmosphere was quite different from that of her previous visits. The noise level was actually tolerable. Nicole released the tension in her shoulders by giving them a quick roll. A few tables were filled with patrons, and a female server kept tabs on them. Nicole's eyes darted in her direction, verifying that it wasn't Liz before she moved to the bar and taking a seat.

The bartender flashed a toothy grin and mopped the bar with a rag. "What can I get ya, hon?" His nametag identified him as Sonny.

Nicole ordered a beer and then drummed her fingers on the bar while she waited for it. She swung her head toward the doorway where Liz seemed to loiter when she wasn't busy. There was no sign of her. When Sonny set her beer on the bar, she decided to ask him.

"I'm looking for Liz. Is she working tonight?" Nicole sipped her beer, watching him over the rim of her glass.

"Um, sorry, but I don't think I know a Liz. She a friend of yours?"

"Yes. We met here about a week ago. I was supposed to come by on Tuesday night, but I got caught up at work. Are you new here?"

He shook his head. "No, actually, I've been working here over five years. Are you sure her name is Liz? What does she look like?"

Nicole thought for a moment as she sipped her beer. "Mmm, well, she has pitch-black hair...not dark brown, black as night...and the bluest eyes...they're very striking. She's beautiful. You'd notice her."

Sonny smiled as he grabbed a towel and began wiping the bar. "Is it possible she goes by Elizabeth?"

Nicole thought about that for a second. "I guess it's possible, but she introduced herself to me as Liz." An uneasy feeling began to grow in Nicole's belly. Had Liz played her?

"Uh huh," the bartender replied. "Does she wear an old-style barmaid's outfit? Blouse kind of low cut and frilly?"

Nicole's relief was evident in her sigh. "Yes! So you do know her."

Sonny nodded. "Hold on a sec." He went into a back room and came out holding a small photograph, which he placed in his breast pocket. He drew himself a beer before coming around the bar to sit next to Nicole. He sipped the beer, then removed the photo from his pocket and held it out. "Is that her?"

Nicole took the worn black and white photo, which had seen better days. The edges were frayed, and the image was faded. She studied the photo—two women standing together in what looked to be the Rusty Rudder Tavern, but many years ago. She stared at the women, both in barmaid garb, their arms around each other's waist, and smiling for the camera. Both were beautiful. One of them had blond hair, and the other, hair so dark it could be no other shade than blackest black. Nicole looked closer. The black haired woman looked a lot like Liz.

"What is this?" She swallowed hard and set the photograph on the bar. "Is this Liz's mother?"

Sonny shook his head and pulled the picture to him. "No, it's not her mother." He tapped his finger on the dark-haired barmaid. "That's Elizabeth. And you're not the first person that has come in here over the years looking for her." He swigged his beer.

Nicole's brow furrowed as she tried to process what he was saying. "I don't understand. How could that be Liz in that old photo?"

He smiled then and turned toward her with obvious relish for his tale. "Elizabeth was a barmaid who worked here a long time ago, long before you or I were born."

"What?" Nicole sputtered.

Some of the patrons looked Nicole's way in reaction to her

outburst.

"Let me finish," he continued. "I know this is a lot to take in, but you're not the first person I've had this conversation with."

A fine film of sweat formed along Nicole's forehead and the back of her neck. The conversation felt surreal.

"Despite her being a married woman, Elizabeth was said to be a very flirtatious employee of the Rusty Rudder. She was beautiful and she knew it, and she knew that flaunting her...wares would get her better tips. However, not everyone appreciated her outgoing nature, especially her husband. They say she had a pretty torrid affair with the other woman in this photo." Sonny tapped the blonde in the photo to underscore his recital. "Mary, her name was. Well, Elizabeth's husband got wind of their relationship, and one night he followed her to work. He killed her in a jealous rage, back there." The bartender tilted his head toward the back hallway. "The story says that he meant to kill them both, but, lucky for Mary, she wasn't working that night."

Nicole's mouth hung open. *He's gone on one too many ghost tours himself if he believes that story.* She'd kissed Liz. She'd touched her skin and held her hands. The woman she'd met was flesh and blood, not the specter of a woman who had been murdered. And yet, it did appear to be her in the photo.

"Can I see that again?" Nicole held out her hand and Sonny placed the photo in it. She examined it more closely. The raven haired barmaid was a dead ringer for the woman she had kissed just a few nights earlier. There was no doubt; the woman in the photo had to be Liz.

"Uhh, I... I just don't understand what you're telling me. I..."

He tilted his head in her direction and took back the photo.

"Believe me, like I said, you're not alone. Every year, Elizabeth comes back and...interacts with a patron, although this is the first time I've heard that she referred to herself as Liz. She shows up on nights when the moon shines brightly in the sky. And always right before Halloween, which was when old Jim killed her."

Nicole squinted. The two nights she had seen Liz, the moon had been glowing brightly. Even on the night of the ghost tour, when rain threatened, the clouds had parted enough for the moon to shine through.

"After Halloween," Sonny continued, "she disappears for another year. We've had several people over the years saying that they had some romantic encounters with her out back."

Goosebumps rose on Nicole's skin. Not wanting to admit that she'd been physical with what now seemed likely was a ghost, she tried to hide her reaction. The thought made her feel ill.

"You should take the ghost tour they operate here in town. They come in here and tell you the whole story. It's really something." The bartender's weathered face was transformed by his sympathetic smile. "I have to get back to work, but let me get you another beer while all this sinks in for you." He rose and moved back around the bar.

Nicole thought back to the evening of the ghost tour. She had gone to the restroom and so had missed the tale about the ghost that haunted the tavern. When she left Liz in the ladies room and came back out to the pub to join her friends, she remembered Danni saying that something interesting had happened at the bar, but she'd never gotten around to telling her what that was.

She fumbled her cellphone out of her pocket and hit speed dial for Danni as Sonny placed the second beer on the bar in front of her.

Danni answered on the second ring. "Yo, cuz. What's up?"

"Danni, tell me the story from the ghost tour about the Rusty Rudder."

"Well, hello to you too, friend. What the hell are you talking about?"

"Remember when I came back from the ladies room the night of the tour and you told me something really interesting had happened here? What was the story the tour guide told?"

There was momentary silence on the other end. "That was

the place you met your girl, right?"

"No. I mean, yes, but she's not my girl. What was the story he told?" Nicole squeaked out.

"Oh yeah, I remember. It was pretty cool actually. There was a woman who worked there about a million years ago. Her boss killed her, and she comes back sometimes and plays nicey-nice with somebody in the bar. Why are you asking me about that?"

Nicole could hear Danni's television in the background and focused on that as her ears rang. She didn't know if she was going to be sick or have a panic attack, but either one seemed possible.

"Wait a minute. Is the dead chick your girl? Is she?" Oh my God, she is! I have to tell Steph. She is not gonna frickin' believe this! That's why you're asking, isn't it?"

"So it seems," Nicole answered glumly. *I think I'm going to be sick.*

"Geezus, this is awesome, Nicks! You made out with a ghost! Seriously, when does that ever happen? Did you see her tonight?"

"No, she's gone." Nicole sighed, sorry she'd called Danni. She knew Danni would talk about this for years. "The bartender said that she disappears every year after Halloween. According to the guy at the bar, this happens every year. Danni, I am freaked out about this. I made out with a ghost!"

Nicole looked up to see the patrons watching her. She blushed to think that they had heard her admission. She swiveled the other direction on her barstool and lowered her voice. "I just feel, I don't know, creeped out. What if she haunts me now? Not to mention the fact that I was really into her, and then I find out she's *dead*? What do I do with *that* information, Danni?"

"Man, this is so cool. I wish it would have happened to me. I am going there next year and hanging out in the restroom. Steph will just have to give me a free pass for a couple of nights, because I am not gonna miss that opportunity!"

Nicole rested her head in her hand. "Danni, I've got to go.

I have to process this. I'll talk to you soon." Danni was still talking when Nicole pushed the "end" button. She flagged Sonny and asked for her check.

"You okay? I know it's a lot to take in, but like I said, you're not the only one."

Nicole didn't know if that reminder made her feel better or worse. "I'll be okay. I need to run to the ladies room, but I'll pay the tab as soon as I get back."

Nicole hurried through the pub area and into the restroom. She stood by the counter in front of the mirrors and gazed around the room, looking for any sign that Liz had been there. The bathroom seemed cavernous without Liz's warm presence. Numbed by what she had learned from Sonny, her eyes filled with tears. *I knew I should have just stayed home with Tater that night. Anytime I break away from the norm, something bad happens.*

When she had finished in the stall, she returned to the common area and plodded to the first sink. She was washing her hands when she smelled the familiar spicy scent she'd associated with Liz. Her head jerked up and she spun around, but no one else was in the room. Turning back toward the sink, she looked up into the mirror, and gasped. The glass was frosted over with steamy moisture, and written in the mist was a brief message: "You were different."

Nicole was in the hospital's central supply room, gathering stock for the storeroom up front. Her arms were laden with boxes of gauze and latex gloves.

Laughter echoed down the hall, and Nicole tilted her head to listen. *Laughter, at this time of the evening? That* is *unusual.* Most patients were sleeping, so the nurses typically tried to keep noise to a minimum. She bumped the light switch with her elbow and nudged the door closed behind her with her hip, then proceeded down the hall toward the nurses' station. When Nicole turned the corner, she saw that the duty nurses were all in the common area, gathered around a woman.

Nicole stocked the shelves in the supply closet and then returned to the station, all the while wondering who the visitor was. As she drew near to the group, she recognized Elise, one of the patients from the highway pileup the day before Halloween. Her injuries had been severe enough to land her in the hospital for nearly a week, but Nicole was happy to see that the bruising and swelling that had distorted her features during her recovery were gone. Nicole hadn't noticed what an attractive woman Elise was.

All at once, crystal blue eyes turned toward Nicole, along with a brilliant smile.

How did I not notice how black her hair is? Nicole shrugged it off. She had probably come across several women with similar attributes before, but she assumed she was only noticing it now because of her encounters with Liz.

Nicole greeted her with a warm smile. "Elise, how are you?" She was very fond of the patient who, despite her injuries, had never complained or caused any of the hospital staff any grief.

Elise smiled in return, and Nicole felt a warm familiarity in the gesture.

"I'm doing really well, Nicole. I came by to bring you all some things that I baked to thank you for taking such great care of me while I was here." Elise beamed as she gazed at Nicole through her thick eyelashes.

Nicole rubbed her arms as a chill washed over her. "That was very nice of you. How did you know we all have a sweet tooth?" The other nurses were already nibbling on the treats, and Nicole eyed the snacks hungrily.

Elise picked up a nearby plate and offered it to Nicole. "Everyone has a sweet tooth to some extent—that's how I manage to stay in business." At Nicole's confused look, Elise said, "I own a bakery downtown—Sisters' Bake Shop, down by the harbor."

"Oh, wow! Yeah, I know that place. I had no idea you owned it." Nicole examined the selections on the plate before choosing a decadent-looking brownie. "What happened to the bakery while you were laid up?"

Elise shrugged. "My family and staff stepped in and kept it running. I'm so lucky to have them." She hesitated. "I'm lucky just to be alive, I guess, right?" Her eyes were shiny with unshed tears.

Nicole put her half-eaten treat on a napkin and enveloped Elise in a hug. "You're a strong woman, and I'm sure your upbeat attitude helped you heal so quickly." A spicy scent tickled Nicole's senses, one that she knew she would never forget. Her head spun at the familiar scent, and she pulled away from Elise.

Elise dabbed at her eyes. "I'm so very thankful to you all. This was the least I could do."

Each of the nurses in turn came and hugged Elise. Vaguely aware of the others around her, Nicole tried to sort through her confusion. Several of her senses were being assaulted at once. Why did Elise's visit remind her of Liz? After a successful week of barely thinking of Liz, Nicole had hoped that she had put the past month behind her once and for all.

After a few more minutes of chatter, Elise bade farewell to the nurses, and they all returned to work, including Nicole, who couldn't shake the feeling that something in her life had shifted forever.

❧

Later that week, Nicole was working a slow shift at the hospital. No emergencies had brought in additional patients, and the current patients were sleeping or occupied. Nicole was reviewing her work schedule for the next week, when the phone rang.

Susan, the duty nurse, answered. After a brief exchange with the caller, she held the receiver toward Nicole. "It's for you, hon."

Nicole's brow furrowed. She rarely received calls at the hospital. Even when Danni called Nicole while she was on duty, she always called her cellphone. She took the phone from

Susan and held it to her ear. "Hello?"

"Nicole, hi. This is Elise Grant."

Nicole's mouth opened in surprise. "Elise, hi! Is everything okay?"

"Hey, I'm fine." There was a long, almost uncomfortable silence before Elise cleared her throat and then continued. "Um, I've wanted to call you all day, and I have to admit I'm pretty nervous."

"Nervous? Why? What's wrong? Are you having some health issues?"

Elise's nervousness was apparent in her laugh. "No, no, I'm fine. It's not that. It's just that, well…okay, this is going to sound really strange. I'm not normally one of those spacey people who believe in all that cosmic woo woo stuff, but well, I've been thinking about you, and I had a very strange dream last night that had to do with you. I don't usually pay any attention to dreams and things, but this dream was so real. Strangely, it's not the first time I've had the dream, but it's the first time you were in it."

Nicole was intrigued, and the sense of déjà vu again struck her. She tugged on a lock of hair and spun it around her finger. "Do you want to tell me about it?" *Say "no." I'm not sure I want to hear this.*

"Yeah, well, hmmm." Elise drew a deep breath. "Well, for as long as I can remember, I've had this dream that I was someone else, someone who lived a long time ago," Elise said in a very quiet voice. "I haven't ever told anyone about it, because I've never given it much credence and I didn't want anyone to think I was a flake."

The hairs on Nicole's arms stood on end. Part of her didn't want to hear any more of this conversation, and part of her wanted to hurry Elise along. "Okay, and?" Nicole prompted.

Elise blew out a breath. "Anyway, I had the dream again the night I stopped by the hospital, but this time you were in it. We were…well, in the dream, you and I were…we were dating…"

It seemed to Nicole that Elise had paused to see whether

Nicole would react to the statement.

When she didn't, Elise continued. "...and well, in the dream, I told you that you were different. I don't even..."

Nicole dropped the phone. Suddenly lightheaded, she dropped into a nearby office chair.

Susan picked up the phone and held it out to Nicole. "Nicole, is everything okay? Did you get some bad news?"

Nicole rubbed her face with both hands and brushed her long bangs away. The shock was fading, and she knew she had to finish her conversation with Elise. "Yeah, I'm okay. Just got a bit dizzy, I guess."

"Do you need to lie down? Should I tell her you'll call back?" Susan offered, clearly concerned.

Nicole stood and shook her head, reaching for the phone. "No, I'm fine. Just forgot to eat tonight. I'm fine, I promise." She smiled weakly as she clutched the phone to her ear. "Hi. Sorry about that," she said to Elise.

"Are you okay? You dropped the phone, didn't you? Did what I said mean something?" Elise's voice was full of concern.

Nicole fiddled with the phone cord, not sure of how much she should share. "You were different" rang in her head. "Um, yes...yeah, I dropped the phone, but I'm fine. It's just that, what you said...you're not the first person who has said that to me."

Elise sighed. "Listen, would you like to have dinner with me?"

Nicole had to know more. The surreal feelings of the past week had to be connected to her experiences with the spirit of Liz at the tavern. "I would like that very much."

"Good. Great!"

Nicole could hear the smile in Elise's voice.

They made plans to meet over the weekend, then Nicole hung up the phone and rubbed her eyes. It was going to be a long night.

EPILOGUE: ONE YEAR LATER

Nicole held open the door to her apartment so that Danni and Steph could bring in the last of the moving boxes from Danni's pick-up truck. Tater was in a nearby crate, whining to be set free. Nicole sympathized with her dog, but knew that temporary imprisonment was a better alternative than having Tater run off during the chaos of moving.

"Oof!" Danni dropped the box heavily in the dining room. "Dinner had better be good, Nicks. I'm starving. I didn't know your girlfriend had an ungodly amount of possessions that we'd be moving in here!"

Nicole laughed. Many things had changed over the last year, but Danni's flair for the overdramatic was not one of them. She rubbed her friend's back affectionately. "Elise and I appreciate your help, and Steph's help, more than you'll ever know. That being said, you do owe me—we helped you move into Steph's place not six months ago." She patted Danni's bottom.

Elise came up behind Nicole, wrapped her arms around her and rested her chin on Nicole's shoulder. "I especially appreciate it, Danni, and dinner is on me." She kissed Nicole's neck and went to close the outside door so she could free Tater from her prison.

Nicole turned and watched her, her heart filled with love. The past year had been incredible. It had been clear during their first dinner together that they were officially on a date. Despite the disturbing dream Elise had shared with Nicole, there was a strong attraction between the two, and the date had been the first of many. Nicole had related her experiences at the Rusty Rudder Tavern, expecting the tale to be greeted with disbelief. She was instead pleased to find that Elise believed the entire story. After many conversations, they had come to the conclusion that Liz had somehow served as matchmaker. Elise took the supposition one step further; she believed that she might be a reincarnation of Liz—a viewpoint Nicole wasn't yet ready to believe.

"All right, starry eyes," Danni teased. "Let's grab some grub."

Nicole smiled and grabbed her car keys from the table. Since it had held such a significant place in her heart, they were going to the Rusty Rudder for dinner. Nicole hadn't been back to the pub for a year, not since the night she'd heard Sonny's story about Liz, and she was anxious to take Elise to the pub to see if her girlfriend picked up any vibes.

"Let's go, girls," she called. She released Tater from her crate and patted her on the head. "I'll bring you some tasty leftovers, girl. You be good, and do some unpacking while we're gone."

∽

The Rusty Rudder was moderately busy for a late Saturday afternoon. The four women sat at a table near the bar, enjoying the food as well as each other's company. They were all tired from a full day of moving, but Nicole was on high alert. Her senses prickled, and every time she turned her head, she expected to see Liz.

Nicole patted Elise's hand and excused herself to visit the ladies room. She took a deep breath and blew it out slowly before she entered, prepared for a possible encounter even though it was after Halloween and the legend of Liz specifically stated that she only appeared during the month of October. Nicole went to the row of sinks and placed her palms on the counter. Leaning in, she gazed at herself in the mirror. "Well, I guess you're gone for good."

She returned to the main room, stopped at the bar, and flagged the bartender, an older gentleman who looked like he had been behind the bar for decades.

"What can I get for ya, darlin'?"

"I don't need a drink, but I was hoping I could talk to you

about Liz, uh, Elizabeth," she said tentatively, not sure how her request would be received.

He smiled broadly. "Elizabeth! Well, I am an expert on all things Elizabeth. I've worked here for the past twenty years and have heard many, many stories. What would you like to know?" He planted his elbow on the bar and rested his chin on his hand.

"Mmm, well, I'm wondering if there have been any new, uh...sightings, I guess you'd say. I haven't been here in a while, but I know that she appeared last year."

The bartender stood upright with excitement. "Oh yeah, you're right about that. I hear that Elizabeth showed up last year and broke some poor girl's heart. She worked her wiles on her and then disappeared like she does every year."

Nicole's face flushed, and she hoped that the bartender would not figure out he was speaking with the "poor girl" whose heart Liz had broken.

"But it looks like Elizabeth may have moved on," the bartender observed.

Nicole's eyes grew round.

"Yeah," he continued, "maybe her heart was broken as well, or maybe she finally found peace, but Elizabeth has not appeared at all this year. As far as I know, that's a first. At least it's a first in the twenty years I've been working here. Lots of people were actually disappointed that there haven't been any sightings, but I like to think that Elizabeth has finally found peace, for whatever reason. I love this bar, but it's no place for someone to spend eternity, you know what I mean?"

Nicole nodded absently. What did all of this mean? Had Liz indeed moved on because Nicole and Elise had found each other, or was it coincidence? Nicole was sure they were somehow related. She glanced over at her table.

Elise was watching her, a concerned smile on her face. Suddenly her smile grew, and Nicole marveled as Elise's blue eyes seemed to sparkle with clarity, then turned a foggy color before returning to their normal shade.

As she strode toward Elise, Nicole clearly heard a voice in

the air say, "You *are* different."

Nicole smiled, grateful to Liz for bringing Elise into her life, and happy for Liz, as well, knowing without a doubt that the spirit was finally at peace.

〜

AUTHOR'S NOTE

I would like to thank my wife Angela for being my biggest cheerleader. In her eyes, I can do no wrong (at least as a writer!) Thanks as well to my friend Katina Lear, who read an early draft of the story and gave me suggestions for a better, more dramatic ending. And finally, thank you to Astrid Ohletz, the best coach a writer could ask for, and to Day Petersen, who polished the story with her editing skills.

WOLF MOON
by Erzabet Bishop

INDSAY PORTIS GROANED INWARDLY as she surveyed the expo hall full of masked avengers, geeked out teens, and caped crusaders. *Crap*. Why had she let Jenna talk her into coming? Jenna had been babbling about some band that Lindsay just *had* to hear, but God, why pick this place to hear them? Lindsay loved a good Halloween party more than anything, but not one that was a mob scene being held at the convention center. Especially since it seemed like it was a combination Monster/Comic event.

There were kids running everywhere, but what stunned her were the adults. Dressed to the extreme in spandex and leotards, it was obvious some of them were not even remotely functioning in the world of reality. *Like that guy.*

She shook her head at a man in a really ugly Wookie costume and smiled to herself as a gaggle of kids all outfitted in the same light up tee shirt streaked past. *Halloween party meets the geek squad.* Oh, Jenna was going to pay for this one.

The ratio of costumed characters to young adults in geek wear actually surprised her. She had expected all of the attendees to be decked out in Superman capes and Wonder Woman bustiers. Instead, it was about a 50/50 mix.

The Halloween decorations made her smile too. Coffins and animatronic zombies twitched and moaned in a graveyard setup, and a badly made up Dracula tried to bite some of the young women as they walked by. Classic Halloween and monster-themed tunes were being piped in through speakers overhead, and Lindsay found herself humming "Monster Mash" as she walked along. She'd had a date with a smut novel and a fresh box of chocolates, but Jenna's pleading had convinced her that coming to this party would be more fun. *"Come on, Linds! You might meet someone. You never know."*

Lindsay harrumphed and kept walking. Most of the women she knew were straight, and she wasn't one to arrange a date online. You just never knew for sure who you were talking to. Add to that her crazy schedule as a retail bookstore manager, and the usual date nights and get-togethers were out. She worked a lot of nights. But Jenna had begged so nicely, that Lindsay had finagled her schedule to help her friend.

Jenna was fearless in every other aspect of her life. She was just totally afraid to go alone to large group gatherings like parties and conventions. Last year Jenna had dragged her to a cat convention, and Lindsay had gone home with enough cat toys and kitty litter to last three years. God only knew what she was going to bring home from this one.

As she made her way past a booth for a comic book store called "Look A Palooza," Lindsay sighed and shook her head. Kids were swarming all the booths, buying comic books, light sabers, and posters. Lindsay supposed she shouldn't judge them, given her own penchant for smut novels, but still, some things were an affront to nature. Like kids not even old enough to shave clutching hundred dollar bills, while she had barely enough change in her purse to afford a couple of tacos at Taco Banana later. It was also annoying that she'd had to pay for parking and then pay to get in. *That is coming out of Jenna's hide when I catch up to her.* This was a "venti salted caramel mocha with a cream cheese pumpkin muffin" kind of pain-in-the-ass day, and she was so going to need the chocolate coffee bliss by the time she got out of there.

Looking around for any sign of her soon-to-be-dead friend, Lindsay shrieked in outrage as two guys in stretch pants plowed into her, sending her reeling head first into a large theme-oriented display of plants and tombstones. Slamming her shin against the surprisingly hard plastic, Lindsay yowled as her face met with a large ficus. "Ow!"

"He's got a gun!" one of the teens shouted as he ran, cape fluttering behind him.

Lindsay gaped after him, flailing against a particularly persistent plant that whapped her in the face. *A gun? Holy shit. No way.* It had to be a re-enactment. They couldn't have a bunch of Caped Crusaders without a bad guy. It was all just fun and games, after all. Lindsay was sure that they did stuff like that all the time at these kinds of things.

After scraping herself out of the moss and foliage, Lindsay found herself in the middle of another stampede as three teens came running in her direction screaming about the crazy guy with a gun. She had just enough time to jump back into the plants so she didn't get trampled a second time as they raced for the exit. *Yeah, right. If anybody does have a gun, they'd better keep it away from me, because right now, I could happily grab it and use it on those damn kids knocking everybody down in their role playing.*

She disengaged herself from the fully leafed ficus, smoothed down her tee shirt, and brushed off her shorts. Advancing into the expo hall, she heard more screams. A spike of anger stabbed through her. Of course there were going to be guns; it was a super hero costume event and a Halloween party. Guns and swords and light sabers were strapped on half the costumed population in there.

She rolled her eyes and stalked down the carpeted walkway toward the main hall. "Love Potion #9" began to play, and Lindsay hummed along, trying to squelch her irritation. After all, it was a party. She should at least try to have some fun.

The burst of yelling and noise off in the distance to her left sounded just a little too real. Lindsay bit her lip and growled as she scanned the crowd. Being a manager at a bookstore, she'd had her share of weirdoes and countless incidents, including robberies, over the years. She could pretty much tell when something was wrong, and her radar was pinging. If Jenna was in there, Lindsay had to find out what the hell was going on. After this, they were so having a discussion about meeting at Starbucks the next time. Lindsay had enough drama at the bookstore. Days off should be quiet. With coffee, smut books, and chocolate. And in that order, too.

She moved to a secluded corner, whipped out her phone,

and sent Jenna a text.

✍

"All units, all units. Shots fired in Expo Building Side 1A. I repeat, shots fired in Expo Building, Side 1A. Subject not visible. Shots fired. Snipers stand down. SWAT notified. Taggert, report."

Taggert's insides clenched when the call came in. A gunman was active and roaming the Comic Art Con Halloween Extravaganza. It was believed that one person had been shot already.

Great. Taggert strapped on her vest and made sure her gun was locked and loaded. She was the one they sent in when snipers couldn't get a bead on the suspect. Like now. It was her turn.

"Taggert on site and going in," she replied into the police radio. She crept closer to one of the service doors at the side of the hall where the gunman was last reported.

The hallway was dimly lit and led straight into the main ballroom of the conference hall. She could see booths set up in the center and pulled out the map the sergeant had given her. The event had one hundred and fifty booths, a movie exhibit, and a stage where a band was scheduled to play later in the afternoon. She looked at her watch and grimaced. Two hours until the band was to perform and the place was already crawling with people, most of them in costume. She needed to secure the subject with as little collateral damage as possible.

Taggert moved quietly, trying to blend in with the crowd until she found what she was looking for. The screaming was hard to miss. In the corner next to the stage, near the entrance to the small onsite bank, the perp was holding a small crowd of convention goers. Taggert saw that a tall, youthful male with an air of authority was presiding over the hostages. Restless energy rolled off of the gunman as he paced back and forth like a caged animal. The closely cropped dark hair was neatly trimmed, the skin pulled taut over the ridge of high cheekbones. His shoulders were broad, and his form muscular. Jaw clenched, he had a stubborn, arrogant look about him. His posture was aggressive as he held a gun on the group.

"On the floor! All of you. *Now!* You!" He aimed his weapon at a teenage boy in a vampire costume. "Get that bank manager over here, and tell him to bring the money." His gun waved wildly toward a man behind the counter in the bank and gestured him to come out, but the man wasn't moving.

One of the girls near the counter collapsed in tears. A security officer stepped forward. His voice was so soft that Taggert couldn't hear what he said. The guard gesticulated with his hands, trying to get the gunman to stand down. The boom of gunfire echoed in the cavernous space. Falling to the floor, the security officer screamed as blood spread across the pant leg of his khaki uniform.

"I told you to get down, people! Now do it! The next asshole who doesn't listen to me is dead. Do you understand?"

More screams erupted in the hall as a random shot echoed through the space. A man beside the sobbing girl grabbed her arm and dragged her back into the anonymity of the crowd.

"Look around, people. Do you see the black duffle bag next to the bank counter?" The gunman gestured toward the bank. Several people turned their heads to look. "Good. You are paying attention." His features twisted into a smirk, his eyes cold and flat. "If the bank manager doesn't give me what I want, you're all are going to find out what's in the bag."

His dark rolling laugh set the hair on Taggert's arms on end. *Unfucking real. What is in the bag?*

Taggert fell back to a location where she could still see what was happening while she considered how best to get the situation under control. As soon as she got to a safe place, she had to radio in and let the team know of the latest developments.

She looked over the map and then moved away from the gunman toward an area where there was supposed to be a service entrance. Crouching low and keeping an eye on the suspect, she backed into the hallway. As she did, out of the corner of her eye she saw a second gunman appear at the entrance of the bank. Taggert watched in dismay as he reached down into the duffle bag and pulled out what appeared to be a homemade bomb.

"Okay Mr. Bank Manager," the gunman cooed, hefting the bomb. "If you don't want this crowd blown to kingdom come, you better get your ass back there and get that safe open, or we're going to have to get rough." When the bank manager still did not comply, the young man looked around among the hostages. "Maybe we should make an example of this young woman here."

Chiseled features morphed into a predatory smile as he moved toward one of the captives.

"You." The second gunman pointed at a young blond woman with a bank name badge fixed to her blouse. "Get over here now."

"But…I…" The woman froze, her face a mask of panic.

"Now, bitch." He yanked her toward the bank counter. He pulled a roll of duct tape from the bag on the ground and proceeded to wrap the homemade pipe bomb to the woman's abdomen.

Her sobs carried across the room, and Taggert had to fight the urge to shift and take the motherfucker out right then. If she did, Graham would hand her her head in a bag, and she would be out of a job she loved. No, she had to bide her time.

"Now, where are you, Mr. Manager? You so chicken shit that you let your employee here take the heat for you? You have twenty minutes to get the money to me, or this lovely lady is going to become a pile of blood and guts right here, along with most of the rest of you. We want the money. We'll leave you to it. Your time starts now." He pushed a button on the device and a beeping sound filled the shocked silence. The bomb was activated.

The bank manager paled and vanished into the recesses of the bank. Taggert hoped the safe didn't have a time lock. A lot of banks used those these days for just that reason.

"Twenty minutes. Fuck."

❦

When Lindsay heard the first shot from close by, she almost wet herself. It wasn't a joke. There was a real jerk with a gun out there, and he had staked out the stage where the concert was to be held. She rounded the corner and saw the gunman freaking out. When she spotted the service entrance, she ducked through it, trying to figure out what she should do, how she could find Jenna.

She looked back into the room through the small glass window, thankful she could watch while hidden from view. She nearly cheered as someone wearing a bulletproof vest approached the door. It seemed likely that it was a cop in plain clothes. Ass first, the cop backed toward the same safe space Lindsay was occupying.

The door eased open, and Lindsay was staring right at the well-shaped, jean-clad derriere. She almost reached out to touch the vision of taut loveliness, but sighed as caution reared its head. Who knew what was on the other side of that coin? Even if this turned out to be a girl who liked the ladies, there were far more pressing considerations at the moment. Lindsay fell back onto her ass, and a burst of air whooshed from her lips as the cold concrete floor made contact through her shorts. Still, she rather hoped the face matched the gorgeous rear view, because anything less would be a crying shame.

Lindsay sighed and pursed her lips. "You want to get your ass out of my face?"

The startled officer spun around, and in an instant Lindsay was staring past the barrel of the gun to a pair of silver blue eyes.

The officer's eyes narrowed. "Don't move."

Lindsay held out her hands and scooted away, trying not to think about the fact that the gorgeous cop probably had handcuffs on her utility belt. A girl could dream.

❦

Life had been a series of bitch slaps lately, and this was another one. It was staring at Taggert in the form of a petite little redhead in a tight white tee shirt and form fitting shorts. Another redhead. *Holy Christ. Not today.*

The ink wasn't even dry on the divorce papers her wife had served Taggert after she had been infected with the lupine virus. "For better or for worse" had decidedly gone in the latter direction, and Shelby had bailed after she had witnessed Taggert changing that first time. It didn't matter that Taggert would never have hurt her. Ever. All that mattered to Shelby was being normal. Human. Like everyone else. Taggert could be a lesbian and a cop, but not a monster. That was an unforgivable crime, and Shelby had never let her forget it.

And now here she was eyeing this girl. No. Woman. The redhead was very much a woman. Taking in the soft globes of her breasts and the way the shirt was painted on her like a second skin made Taggert want to forget the gunmen, the bomb, her responsibilities, and bury her face in that chest and just stay there.

The bite wound on her arm from the shifter attack had healed, but the moon was due to be full tonight. Her heightened senses and boiling blood were going wild. In this closed space, she could scent the girl's arousal. It reached deep inside, the need scraping her senses to the core and then filling them back in with the essence of the woman. She had the sense that this was someone who could make her whole again.

My mate.

Just looking at the woman at her feet made her want to do things she hadn't considered since Shelby had stopped warming her bed. God, it felt like a thousand years ago. They had been on the outs well before the issues with Graham began, Taggert just hadn't wanted to believe it. When she became infected with the lupine virus, that was the last straw for Shelby.

Taggert closed her eyes and gave herself a mental shake. That time was over. There was a gorgeous woman in front of her that was striking a chord deep inside of her. Shaking with her hunger, she struggled to maintain control. *Down, girl.* Her beast was ravenous; it scented a potential mate in the woman on the floor.

Could it be? A mate? Here? Now?

Taggert's nipples tightened. Lust clouded her vision, and she almost forgot why she was there in the first place. *Damn it.* She definitely didn't need this distraction. She staggered to the wall and willed her traitorous body back under control. Gunman first; imaginary sex with gorgeous redheaded woman later.

"Move away from the entrance, Red."

The young woman smirked at her and eyed her with a hungry look that made Taggert's body scream in frustration. *Control!*

Totally ignoring Taggert's instruction, the girl got up from the floor and moved toward the window. "Is he still there?"

"Stay back." Taggert holstered her gun and peered through the window into the convention hall. She pulled out her radio and tried to push the girl away from the door and further back into the hallway. "Please stay back. I don't want you to get hurt."

The girl crossed her arms under her breasts.

"Taggert here. Suspects located." The radio crackled, and she turned down the volume.

"Confirmed. Status?"

"Two gunmen. One at the concert stage, the other at the bank entrance. They're waiting for the bank manager to bring the money. What appears to be a homemade explosive device has been duct taped to a bank teller. The second suspect gave the manager twenty minutes to get the money, or he will detonate the bomb. I need SWAT and the bomb squad on site stat."

There was a crackle on the line, and a new voice joined the conversation. "Taggert, this is Sergeant Graham."

"Sergeant." She struggled to keep her voice even. That bastard had no right to interfere in her operation, especially given the bullshit he had pulled with her wife. He had encouraged Shelby to leave her and then made his move. Hell. He was in her bed a long time before the divorce was even final. There was a special place in Hell for people like Graham. A slow, poisonous hate churned in the pit of her stomach, and she tried unsuccessfully to tamp it down.

"SWAT is on their way. Wait for backup. What kind of bomb?"

"It looked to be a pipe bomb. If it blows, we're going to lose a lot of hostages along with the two suspects."

"Roger that. Wait until the bomb squad is in position before you try to take down the perps."

Anger burned in her gut. *Wait?* She had taken out criminals in every stage of a siege, and Graham was telling her how to run her scene? *Fuck him.* It was two kids with guns…and a bomb. It was the bomb that gave her pause. Could she take out the asshole with the button before he could press it? She knew that she needed the bomb squad to defuse the bomb, but maybe she could at least apprehend the gunmen.

"Sir, with all due respect, the gunmen have already shot at least one person—"

"No. You listen, Detective. Stay where you are. SWAT and the bomb squad are en-route, but there is an accident on the bridge. They will rendezvous with you in about thirty. Stay put. Invisible. You got me? And no fucked up werewolf antics either."

Thirty? Is he kidding? "With all due respect, 'about thirty' doesn't get them here within the gunman's deadline. I don't know if he would seriously blow himself up along with the hostages if the deadline isn't met, but—"

"Taggert!"

"Yeah. I've got you, *Sir.* Staying put. Taggert out." Unable to contain her frustration, she threw the radio against the wall and it clattered to the floor with a reverberating thud.

The sexy cop was having a meltdown. No. The sexy werewolf detective. It figured. More and more weres were being outted all the time. Next it would be vampires. The world was getting more accepting. Why not? She had read enough shifter smut novels to give her lots of ideas about just how wild they could be in bed. Whatever was happening in the convention hall, there were some distinct undercurrents in the exchanges between the two police officers, but that was not her business.

A bomb squad? Her pulse raced, and she moved closer to the window. How could the police possibly take thirty minutes to get there? It was insane. Hadn't the detective just said something about twenty minutes before a bomb would be detonated? *Crap!*

Lindsay stared at the radio on the floor and gave the detective a pointed look. "So, Detective...Taggert, is it? You weren't going to tell me there was a second guy out there with a bomb?"

"You heard me just now. What more do you want?"

"I don't know." Lindsay shook her head. "I can't believe they have to bring in a bomb squad. What if they don't make it in time? My friend is in there somewhere." Her voice choked off as she made a move to get a clear view through the window.

"No!"

Taggert held up a hand, her steel blue eyes flashing a warning that Lindsay was determined to ignore. Or were the eyes yellow? Lindsay stared, not quite believing what she was seeing. "Your eyes..." She tried to mask the uneasy tone in her voice, but it quavered just the same. "They just changed."

It wasn't like having werewolves among them was any surprise, but this was the first time that Lindsay had met one. As far as she knew. This was different from seeing a story on the news or reading smoking hot stories about steamy shapeshifters. This was real, and the sexy shifter was only a couple of feet in front of her.

"I don't know what you're talking about." Taggert snorted,

edging Lindsay away from the window and back into the recesses of the hallway.

Lindsay crossed her arms over her chest and stared, her lips pressed together in anger. "Are you calling me a liar?"

Taggert sighed. "No." She turned from the window and moved toward her. "Look, Red, it will be half an hour before the squad will be here. Maybe less. Let's just stay calm and make the best of this, okay?"

"How do you propose we do that? Whip out a deck of cards?"

"No." She snorted. "I mean. I didn't exactly plan on being stuck here with a civilian while I wait for some asshole to get his squad in gear and make arrangements for this three ring circus. They promoted Graham. Let him worry about the specifics. I'd rather be *in* the shit than organizing all the departments and getting them to try and work together without shooting each other."

"Oh, so now I'm in the same league as the asshole, is that it? A deviation in your freaking master plan?" Lindsay snarled. "Look, my friend is in there. I can't just let her get shot or blown up by a couple of wannabe thugs. I *won't*." She marched toward the door, but Taggert was faster.

"Stop." Taggert knocked her backwards and then pressed her against the concrete wall.

Initially forceful, the move turned into something else as Lindsay stared into the detective's stormy blue eyes. The yellow shifted in and out, but she was prepared for it this time, and it didn't frighten her.

Taggert's body pressed Lindsay to the wall, and the yellow flecks gleamed golden as the were inched to the fore. "You have the softest skin," Taggert whispered, her fingers releasing their hold on Lindsay's wrists.

Sighing, Lindsay let her body relax against the wall. When Taggert's lips brushed against hers, Lindsay met her halfway. The alpha femaleness of the detective pervaded her senses. Lindsay felt the carefully constructed walls she had built around herself start to crumble. It had been so long since anyone had touched her. At all. She hadn't dated in what seemed like forever. To feel the warmth of another soft female form was like handing an éclair to a dieting woman. She wanted it, and she wanted it *now*. Heat pulsed between her legs, and a tear slipped out, unheeded.

"Don't cry. I may hate that sonuvabitch Graham, but he has a bomb squad unit under his command that can take care of any explosive device. The SWAT guys know their stuff, too. They know the bomber's time frame, and they'll get here. We'll get you and your friend out of here safely." Taggert enveloped Lindsay in her arms.

The soft curves of Taggert's breasts pressed against her, and Lindsay trembled with a whirlwind of desire such as she had never felt before. And she knew that this was a moment that would never come again. She was trapped in a secluded place with a cop that looked like something out of one of her erotic daydreams. She lifted her eyes to meet Taggert's, and she knew she had to take a chance. She needed to feel Taggert's hands on her flesh, her fingers inside of her. Right here, right now, Lindsay wanted her with every fiber of her being.

Another round of gunfire erupted in the convention hall, and Lindsay cursed the shooter. A few feet away, men with guns were holding people hostage, and, given the threat of the bomb, they could all die. The danger of the situation only made Lindsay want to feel more alive. The strength and vulnerability that warred in Taggert's eyes made Lindsay's heart flutter in her chest. She believed that things happened for a reason. Sucking in her breath, she stared into the werewolf's yellow eyes and parted her lips in invitation.

Taggert pressed her lips against Red's, and the arousal that had been torturing her rose up like the seething monster it was. The sensation of Red's breasts rubbing against her own snapped the fragile control she was holding over herself. Taggert's nipples pebbled and liquid seeped from her aching slit. She devoured the offered lips like a starving woman. Taggert's hands fisted in the red hair, and her knee thrust willing legs apart as she pressed Red flat against the wall. Kissing and licking down the side of her neck, Taggert yanked up the tee shirt and cupped the luscious breasts in her palms. "Are you sure about this?" she whispered in Red's ear.

Taggert didn't have sex with strangers in hallways. This was not who she was, but for that moment, her body was answering to a stronger force.

This woman is my mate.

Warmth flooded through Taggert, blood pounding insistently through the most sensitive spots of her body. Never had she felt a connection with a woman so quickly. It staggered Taggert and humbled her at the same time—the trust in Red's eyes, even knowing what Taggert was and what could happen if the moon dictated that it was time for her to change. Would she be the monster Shelby thought she was? *No*, she decided. *Not ever.*

The scent of Red's arousal pulled at her. All she knew of the moment was the woman in front of her. She was the world. Gunmen be damned, Taggert needed to taste her, devour her sweetness and keep the darkness at bay.

"Oh yes. I'm sure." Mischief winked in the redhead's eyes. "Better hurry, though. We haven't much time."

Taggert rolled her eyes. "Salacious. That's what you are." She kissed the tempting mouth, exploring it with care. Red was so soft. What began as a feather touch morphed into a burning want, and Taggert had to stifle a moan. She reached between them and, with a flick of a finger, unlatched the bra, releasing the soft mounds into her eager hands. "God." Her lips grazed over the creamy flesh, and she used her teeth to tease Red's nipples into rosy peaks of desire.

"Ohhh."

A moment of clarity flared through fevered brain, and Red pulled herself away from Taggert's ministrations.

"Red?" Taggert stared into the sapphire depths. "I don't even know your name. We're working strictly on chemistry here."

"Lindsay." She smiled and pressed her lips against Taggert's.

∽

Lindsay felt Taggert's tentative touch against the front of her shorts. With shaking fingers, Lindsay hastily unbuttoned them, then slid them down her legs and kicked them to the side. Taggert was sexual desire personified, and Lindsay shuddered in anticipation. The cool air felt erotic against the dampness of her panties, but in seconds, they had joined the shorts on the floor. She shucked the bra as she yanked the shirt over her head, now completely naked and at Taggert's mercy. It felt so amazing—to be touched like this, to be worshipped.

Taggert was still fully clothed. Lindsay watched as Taggert she took off the bulletproof vest and her gun, then laid them on the floor next to Lindsay's clothes. Lindsay's fingers skimmed Taggert's button fly as she pressed her lips against the detective's. Her tongue swirled into the cop's mouth, to mate with hers.

"Oh my God, I need you." Lindsay ran her hands down Taggert's sides, totally turned on that she was naked while her partner was still fully clothed.

Taggert gave Lindsay a light kiss and spun her around to face the wall. "Hands in front of you, and spread your legs."

The authority in Taggert's voice was compelling, and it made Lindsay's pussy weep with need Lindsay positioned her hips and arched her back. Her fingers slid along the concrete wall as she braced herself. She moaned as the material of Taggert's jeans rubbed against her sensitive skin. The anticipation was killing her.

∽

Taggert was so aroused, she couldn't decide what to do first. With Lindsay positioned in front of her, she let her eyes roam over the creamy, smooth skin. Taggert reached around Lindsay and caressed her breasts. Moving her hands lower, Taggert's fingers caressed a sensual path down her abdomen, mapping, exploring, only to finally delve into the delta between Lindsay's thighs. Taggert brushed the mound covered with crinkly red hair, and then slipped a finger inside of Lindsay's pussy, the silky folds slick with desire. She withdrew her finger, and Lindsay mewled in protest.

"Oh, Red. You are so wet. Such a naughty, naughty girl."

"Taggert, *now*. I can't wait any longer. I need you." Lindsay groaned and spread her legs wider, keening softly as Taggert eased two fingers inside of her and began to thrust.

Taggert finger fucked her, thumbing her clit as she stroked, and it wasn't long before the luscious redhead was shuddering in her arms. Taggert wanted more time, but gunfire echoed in the event hall, and there was no more time. Not for the redhead, and certainly not for waiting. It was time to move.

∽

Lindsay's head rested against the wall, her body still spasming in orgasm. Her muddled consciousness realized something was going on. When the shouts came, she felt Taggert pull out of her and heard her move toward the window.

"Lindsay. Here, honey. You need to put these on." She handed Lindsay her clothes.

Lindsay blinked up at her, her mind still muzzy. She jerked upright as a gun went off, and a flood of fear replaced the warmth that had existed inside her only moments before. Now alert, Lindsay put on her bra and yanked the tee shirt over her head, then pulled on her discarded panties and shorts.

Taggert placed a hurried kiss on her forehead. "I need to call in." Taggert grabbed the discarded radio and flicked it on. "Taggert to station. Shots fired. Civilians trapped in range. Perps are still armed. Need ETA on SWAT and bomb squad, ASAP. Report, please."

She looked down at her watch. It had been seventeen minutes. They had better hurry, because if the bomber was serious about the twenty minute deadline, the day was about to get seriously fucked up.

"Detective, SWAT arriving on site. Bomb squad gearing up."

"Taggert going in. Please advise SWAT that a plain clothes officer is in the hall."

"What are you going to do?" Lindsay blinked back tears and jerked her head toward the door as more shots were fired. She had just found the woman who made her feel all the wanton things she had ever dreamed of, and now, as selfish as it seemed, she was most afraid that Taggert could be shot or blown up.

Taggert gave Lindsay a grim look and then placed a light kiss on her lips. "Don't forget, your friend is in there, and she's not the only one." Taggert's eyes caressed the satiated body. "I have to go, babe." She slipped into her gun and vest, and gestured for Lindsay to stay down.

The hell she would!

Taggert tried not to think of the luscious beauty and the amazing sex they had just shared. If she wasn't totally focused, she would get herself shot while being distracted by a curvaceous redhead with a bod built for sin. Taggert's pussy spasmed just thinking about what she wanted to do to her, even now.

Lindsay. My mate.

Reveling in the scent of Lindsay still on her fingers, heat flooded Taggert's body. After this was over, she was going to court her good and proper. A mate. God, it was staggering. She closed her eyes and willed herself to be back into the moment.

Taggert rounded the corner, weapon drawn, and saw the gunman on the stage an instant before he noticed her. She assessed the situation for civilians in danger, and that gave the perp a split second advantage. The force of the bullet rocked Taggert backwards and onto the floor. She roared. Her instinct to protect her prospective mate at all costs took over.

Pain. As her body went into full change, all Taggert was aware of was the buckling sensation of her muscles rippling and altering. Her sense of smell and sight honed to a killing edge. A scream erupted from her throat as a final muscle spasm shook her body to the core, and she writhed in agony and howled in pain.

Moments later, the change complete, Taggert shook off the rags that had been her clothes, and stood up, towering over the humans gathered in front of the stage. Her rage was not directed toward them. No. Only toward the gunmen who threatened what was hers: her mate, her human.

Teeth bared, Taggert snarled as she approached the punk on the stage. The man who had shot her once already screamed as he tried to pull the trigger again as he ran blindly for the exit. This time, she was faster. She lunged toward him and batted the gun from his grip. With her claws, she held him down, daring him to move. The urge to submit to the monster within burbled in the pit of her stomach. Her senses roiled— blood and bone, and the desire to rake across the soft flesh until she uncovered the tender parts beneath.

"Oh God!" he shrieked. "No! Don't fucking eat me!"

The male beneath her reeked of fear, and Taggert drew her lips back in a deadly snarl. His flesh smelled so good, and she wanted to make him pay for shooting her. His scream was high and long, his eyes wide with terror.

A noise from a short distance away caused Taggert to whip her head around. The other perp was emerging from the bank, duffle bag filled to bursting with cash. He had a man in a suit and the woman fitted with the bomb at gunpoint and was herding them toward the outside exit. Seeing Taggert, he shouted. "Oh shit!" Aiming his gun, he fired a round in her direction, but missed.

The woman screamed as the gunman jabbed his gun against her back, then she dissolved into hysterical tears. The man

Taggert surmised was the bank manager tried to drag the teller away, but the shooter put a bullet into the manager's leg.

It was now clear to Taggert that these men wanted the money, but they didn't want to die. The one with the detonator would not explode the bomb and risk his own life.

Taggert raised her paw and bashed the first gunman hard enough to knock him unconscious and, blessedly, his screaming stopped. She had to reach the second perp before he shot someone else or escaped with the money. He was only a few feet away from freedom, and she had no idea where her backup was.

At that moment, the SWAT team broke through one of the plate glass windows, and the man with the money was forced into action. He fired a round that hit Taggert in the thigh, then shoved the blond woman to the floor. As he scrambled toward the exit, money showered from the open bag.

Taggert knew that if the gunman reached the door, he might try to blow the bomb before it could be disarmed in order to cover his escape. Howling her rage, she charged the fleeing gunman, taking him down with a single blow to the side of the head. His gun went skidding across the floor, landing at the feet of a SWAT officer. She ripped the detonator button from his trembling hand. From her vantage point above the would-be bomber, Taggert saw officers in their safety suits removing the device from the blonde, who was still crying and shrieking. Other members of the bomb squad and SWAT team were swarming through the room, evacuating the civilians.

The bank manager was grasping his leg with one hand while trying to stuff the bills back into the bag with the other, but the officers on the scene stopped him so that they could get photographs for evidence. Paramedics were also hovering over the injured man in order to treat his wound. SWAT teams swarmed the first suspect who was unconscious on the floor, and secured him without further incident.

Seeing that the scene was secured, Taggert returned her attention to the man at her feet and growled deep in her throat. The wound in her thigh pulsed as the blood oozed down the matted fur of her leg.

"Get it off me!" the second gunman screamed, his voice shrill. Warm urine stained the front of his jeans. "This *thing* is going to kill me, and you're just going to watch?"

"Detective Taggert, please stop *now*." A nearby SWAT officer was eyeing her warily. "Step away from the suspect. He is officially in custody."

She snarled, unwilling to give up her prey so easily.

"Stand down, Taggert."

She turned her massive frame to see her sergeant shouldering his way through the crowd. The fire of blood lust burned in her veins. It took every ounce of self-control she could muster to tamp it down and not eviscerate the bastard, just for the fun of it. She knew he was fucking enjoying this.

Hating the fact that Graham had seen her change, she concentrated on getting herself under control. It was so new to her; she was still getting used to this body. Taggert had a sudden moment of panic. She didn't want Lindsay to see her like this, not after what had happened between them in the hallway. She didn't want to ruin any chance of wooing Lindsay. Her mate.

As if summoned, the redhead appeared. The rage and anger flooded out of Taggert when her eyes met Lindsay's. All she wanted was to be with Lindsay. Not even Graham, and him stabbing her in the back, mattered.

Taggert groaned as she felt the change begin to reverse, and she hit the floor writhing in pain.

Lindsay gasped as she watched Taggert's body struggling to put itself back to rights. Naked and cold, Taggert was shivering when her human form reappeared. It was agony, watching as her sexy werewolf changed from the proud black haired beast that towered over the humans in the convention hall into the writhing bundle of energy on the floor. Lindsay marveled at what she was seeing, but at the same time, she was terrified.

"Damn it, Taggert! I can't leave you for a single minute without you getting shot!" Scowling, Lindsay glared at a cop standing nearby. "Can we get an EMT over here, please!"

"Just a couple of flesh wounds." Taggert's attempt at a smile turned into a grimace as a final muscle spasm shook her body. "Look, the change has them almost healed already."

"Harrumph." Lindsay snatched a blanket from one of the EMTs who had responded to her summons. She wrapped the blanket around Taggert's strong shoulders, her hands lingering longer than necessary. "Are you done here?"

Taggert sat up and looked around. "I think so. Looks like the SWAT guys and the bomb techs have it wrapped up. Talk about the dumbest crooks ever. Who tries to rob a convention center anyway?"

The medical teams were treating the injured hostages, while the police whisked the two gunmen out of the building, both babbling about a werewolf attacking them. It made Taggert smile.

"Have you found your friend?"

"Not yet. I was a little focused on making sure you hadn't gotten yourself killed." Concern knotting inside her, Lindsay watched Taggert struggle to stand. "Are you sure you can stand? You still look a little off kilter."

"Yes. My head is still trying to adjust back into human mode. As a were, I wanted to rip that guy's head off." Taggert closed her eyes and took a deep breath.

"Which guy?"

Taggert laughed bitterly. "Well, now that you mention it, all of them. But mostly, the sergeant's, if you want to know the truth."

"Is *he* the sergeant?" Lindsay tilted her head toward the man barking orders and directing activity to the left of the stage.

"Yeah. That would be him."

"Why do you hate him so?" Lindsay helped Taggert get to her feet and guided her toward the door and away from the chaos.

"Bastard convinced my ex-wife that my lupine virus made me unfit to be a relationship, and then the sonuvabitch slept with her." Taggert groaned as she took a step forward.

"Are you sure you're okay?"

"Yes. The bullet wounds are healing. One of the perks of the virus. You heal fast, but it kind of smarts."

"Oh." Lindsay sucked in a breath as a frown settled onto her features, then it cleared. "Wow. So, you're divorced then?"

"You could say that."

"Good."

Taggert lifted an eyebrow and gave Lindsay an inscrutable look.

"So, you doing anything later tonight?" Lindsay asked.

"Not really. Why?"

"Your blanket's slipping, by the way."

"Oh!" Taggert laughed, wrapping it tighter around herself. "I hate that aspect of the change. That's the third pair of jeans I've destroyed in the last month."

"Well, that's a pain. I can see it now: Cop arrested for indecent exposure." Lindsay grinned and reached to pull the front of the blanket closed, but not before she got a pleasing eyeful of naked detective. "Do you change with the moon, or does it just happen?"

"Both." Taggert spoke with slight bitterness. "It's damned inconvenient, if you want to know the truth."

"I was kind of thinking...we never did get to finish what we started in the hallway." Lindsay waggled her eyebrows suggestively, hoping Taggert would take the hint.

They pushed through the exit door and outside into the night air.

"Are you sure? Big hairy werewolf? Girl who will use up her quota of razors and hair removal equipment at least once a month? Meat eater. Hates the color pink..."

"I can work with that. Well, except for one thing." Lindsay linked her arm through Taggert's as they slowly walked across the parking lot to her car. "I'm just not sure this would work between us. There might be a deal breaker."

Taggert stopped mid step, her eyes wide. "What?"

Lindsay met Taggert's eyes, her lips twitching with suppressed laughter. "Pink is my favorite color."

Taggert blew out a breath and rolled her eyes. "Oh. I thought you were going to say you didn't date cops or something."

Lindsay giggled. "Yeah, right." She stopped at the car and looked back at the convention center. "You know, before we leave here, I'd better give my friend Jenna a call and make sure she's okay." She pulled her phone out of her purse and checked her text messages. "Well, sonuvabitch."

"Something wrong?" Taggert asked. "She wasn't hurt?"

"Frankly, I'm not sure if I should be mad or insanely grateful."

"What?"

"You know that friend who *begged* me to come here?" When Taggert nodded, Lindsay said, "She never even showed up. She's at home. Something about catching a lupine virus." Lindsay shook her head and grinned up at Taggert.

"Well, I could use some help licking my wounds. What do you say?" Taggert smiled, her gaze as intimate as a kiss.

"I thought you'd never ask."

∿

AUTHOR'S NOTE

For Mom, E. and T. You never stopped believing.

LOVE BITES

by R.G. Emanuelle

"**Y**OU NEED TO GET LAID."

"Yeah?" I replied. "What else is new?"

Cecily and I sat at an airport bar, nursing our drinks as we waited for our flight to New Orleans, where we were meeting our friends for a long Halloween weekend. She looked at me for a while as she ran her finger around the rim of her glass.

"What?" I finally asked.

"By a woman."

"Excuse me?" I glanced around, hoping nobody else at the bar had heard her.

"Sleep with a woman. You look utterly bored. You need to have your boat rocked a little. And that'll do it."

"I—"

"I've done it." She peered over at me as she took a long pull on her screwdriver through a little straw.

"Wha—"

"It was hot." She grinned mischievously. "Don't get me wrong, I still like my ding-dongs, but sleeping with a woman…it really gets your ya-yas out. Know what I mean?"

I pursed my lips, as I usually did at her sophomoric language, and picked up my cosmopolitan. "Um, yeah. I'll think about it." I nervously took a sip. "Look, I know I've been a downer lately, but just being in New Orleans is going to do wonders for me. I love that city. There's just something about it."

Every time I visited NOLA, I'd gotten the sense that there was something else waiting for me, something other than the life I was living. I'd attributed my longings to the atmosphere in New Orleans, the air of abandonment and liberty. Maybe it was the ghosts that haunted the streets of the Big Easy. They tickled people's sensitive spots, awakening slumbering urges and setting ablaze the modest embers of desire and ambition. But I didn't want to tell Cecily that. I didn't think she'd understand.

"I'm telling you," she smiled at a guy in a business suit sitting farther down the bar, "you need something big to shake things up."

Fortified by a few swallows of my cosmo, I decided to confide my desperate desire for change to her. "Okay, you're right. I do need something different. The sameness of my life is squeezing me, like a rope around my chest, and sometimes I can't breathe. It's the same thing, day after day. Same stupid job, same stupid relationships, same stupid everything. I know this sounds strange, but something keeps calling me back to New Orleans." Whatever entities inhabited that city, I felt as if they were trying to free me. For all I knew, it could've been the chicory coffee and beignets, too, but I didn't think so.

With her mouth open and the little straw resting on her bottom lip, she gazed at me for a few moments. "Look," she finally said, "whatever it is you need to do, I'll support you. I've got your back, homey. I know you get wild hairs now and again."

I rolled my eyes and picked up my drink. "Thanks." She was right, though. In an attempt to "shake things up," I had done a few crazy things. But none of them had provided the answer I was looking for.

"I still think you should get laid by a woman."

Little did she know that I'd already been thinking about it. Weird that she would say that to me. Maybe that should have been my first clue that this trip would be different, but I brushed off any anxiety about something weird going down and determined to just have a good time.

❧

We arrived in New Orleans in the early afternoon and met up with our friends. As people tend to do in a place like New Orleans, we went bar-hopping and scoped out the drag and burlesque shows, as well as one show promising live "love acts."

Locals and visitors at the hotels amused themselves by standing on the balconies of the Victorian-meets-Southern plantation structures over Bourbon Street and watching the revelers making fools of themselves. Not that the fools cared. It wasn't unusual to look up and meet someone's eyes— someone who, for whatever reason, found you fascinating at that particular moment. I'd been doing a lot of looking up at strangers that evening, and although I saw no one of note, I had this strange feeling that I should just keep looking, that something was waiting for me high above.

The French Quarter was especially lively, and although it was still two nights before Halloween, people were already decked out in costumes. We had just chugged several daiquiris from one of those places that specialized in them, and were wending our way down the narrow sidewalks of Dauphine, Bourbon, and Royal Streets, skirting knots of other people doing the same thing. On Chartres, a crowd had gathered on the corner and was spilling out into the street. We stopped, not so much because we were interested in what was happening, but because we couldn't easily get around the mob.

"What's going on?" Cecily asked a guy dressed as a nineteenth-century vampire.

"Don't know. Probably somebody getting a free blow job or something."

She giggled. "In public?"

"Honey, this is N'awlins. Anything can happen." He smiled, baring realistic-looking fangs, then he moved off into the crowd.

Cecily squealed in delight, as she pulled me closer. "Did you see that? His teeth were so cool! Maybe we can become vampires while we're here."

"I thought we were just going to sleep with women."

"Well, I already have. But I haven't been a vampire. That would be cool."

"You're nuts." I laughed. Secretly, though, the thought of immortality intrigued me. It *would* be kind of cool. "Besides, vampires don't exist." Unfortunately.

"But it's nice to think they do. Don't you think some people could be vampires? Especially the really sexy ones." She made a low growling sound in her throat, and I laughed. I did have a thing for vampire lore.

While we tried to see what the commotion was about, an unnamable force pulled at me. I glanced up to see who might be looking back, and my breath caught.

Standing on the balcony of a Creole townhouse, a tall, peculiar woman stared down at me. A dark figure, literally. With jet-black hair down to her waist and a long black tunic, she looked as if she'd been born of the night. Even her eyes were dark, reflecting the moonlight like two pieces of polished stone. Her gaze was unsettling, and my spine sparked with a weird lust and warning.

As much as my brain and gut told me to turn away, various other body parts inexplicably wanted to be touched by this frightening, tantalizing woman who had completely bewitched me with just a look. Those body parts, I knew, were going to win.

Her eyes were unflinchingly steady on me, mesmerizing. A new world flashed through my consciousness. I couldn't distinguish any details, but it was a world of freedom and exquisite desires. It was dark, but not bleak. Brimming with clarity, but heavy with burden.

Then she turned away and went inside, and it felt like she'd pulled my soul with her, as if she'd tethered it to her own. Panic coursed through me at the thought that she would not re-emerge.

I wasn't quite sure what to do. I didn't even know whether she lived there. And if she did, so what? I'd knock on her door and do what? Say what? Something like, "Hi. Saw you up there. Do you mind if I take you to bed?" I chewed my lip in frustration.

"Did you see that woman?" I asked Cecily.

"What woman?" Her eyes were drooping, which was understandable after three daiquiris. I doubted at that point that she had seen much of anything.

"The really sexy one."

"A really sexy woman?" Cecily giggled. "Maybe she's a vampire."

An urgent need to find the stranger overwhelmed me.

My other friends were completely oblivious to the epiphany I'd just had. I had to get away from them. Nothing mattered at that moment except finding this woman. "Listen, guys. I'll see you back at the room."

"What? Where are you going?" Cecily asked, slurring her words around a lock of blond hair stuck in her mouth.

I gave her a little grin. "I may be about to take your advice."

Her eyes widened, and she gave me an exaggerated two thumbs up. "You go on with your bad self."

Anxiety shot through me as I realized what I was about to do, but I was helpless against the impulse. "Don't wait up," I said over my shoulder.

The little bar across the street from the house was a great place for a stakeout. I fought for a spot by the window, getting dirty looks from other patrons as I elbowed my way past them. From that vantage point, I had a good view of the house. With my back to the wall to keep pickpockets out of my small backpack, I watched.

All sorts of people in various stages of inebriation went by—some in costume, others not. Two hours passed with no sign of the mystery woman. I was starting to ache—both in longing and in my back.

Then, my heart almost stopped. There she was, emerging from the building. I held my breath, afraid to blink and lose sight of her. She paused momentarily, looked around as if searching for something—but not too hard, then began walking down Chartres Street. Despite my aching back and feet, I quickly pushed my way out of the bar, ignoring the nasty comments I got. I trailed her, trying to keep some distance between us. She turned down Toulouse Street, then made a right on Burgundy and walked several blocks. Then, it was suddenly, eerily quiet.

She walked purposefully, her back straight and her gait confident. I wanted to be just like her, wanted to move with that kind of air. I had her in my sight for another block, and then…she was gone. I ran to the corner and looked both ways, figuring I must have blinked and missed her turning. But it was as if she'd disappeared into the mist. There was no sign of her, not even a rustling from the papers on the ground.

Confused, I stood there, not knowing what to do.

"Why are you following me?"

If one could truly jump out of one's skin, my flesh and skin would surely have parted ways. I spun around and there she was. *How the hell—?*

"What do you want?" Her voice was rich, like thick velvet. Her face, startlingly fair and smooth, was only inches from mine.

I've never been a bold person, but I had a feeling that coyness would get me nowhere with this woman. Were the rules even the same with women? I decided to be blunt.

"You," I said, maybe a little too cockily.

Improbably, her eyes darkened to an even deeper shade—two sleek, perfect gems. They narrowed, and a small grin graced her exquisite red lips. "Well, then. We mustn't disappoint you. Come with me."

Could it be this easy? Since when did things like this happen? I'd have to ask Cecily.

Within a few minutes, we were on the outskirts of the French Quarter. The homes we passed were of a variety of styles and designs, but most had some kind of holiday decoration—*jack-o'-lanterns*, witches hanging from trees, or zombies looking for brains in a garden. The distant sounds of partying rose up again and carried through the night as we walked in silence, me a step behind her. My companion walked smoothly in her tight black pants, the heavy thud her boots made with each step echoing through the drives and alleys.

I followed her through a gate and into a stately Federal-style house, neatly kept, with a widow's walk on the uppermost floor. She guided me through the foyer and into the living room, where she pulled the drapes closed and lit a soft lamp. The furniture was modern, but warm and inviting, and there was an actual brick fireplace—cold at the moment—with several framed photos arranged on the mantel. A vase of orchids perched on a side table, perfuming the room with the scent of toasted coconut and a hint of cinnamon. Underneath that was an unfamiliar scent, one that was slightly pungent, with notes of loam and moss. I sniffed at the orchids, but it wasn't coming from those. I turned slowly to see if I could determine where the smell was coming from. When I turned back to face the interior of the living room, the woman was standing at a bar cart, uncorking a bottle of red wine.

"Would you like some?"

Red wine wasn't my favorite, but at this point, if she had offered me arsenic, I would have accepted it. She could probably talk anyone into anything.

I slowly moved farther into the living room, a little afraid to intrude where I hadn't been invited.

"Please," she prodded. "Don't be shy. Come in."

I went to the center of the large room, where two luxurious black leather sofas flanked a large coffee table that looked as if it was made of ancient stone. She met me there and set the two glasses of wine on the table.

"Sit." She motioned for me to join her on the couch.

I sat down next to her and clutched a wineglass. My hand trembled, and the pulsing between my legs was making it very hard to maintain control. I couldn't believe how lucky I was that this woman was actually going to fuck me—at least, it seemed that way. Then, a small thought crept into my brain: I had no idea who this person was. I mean, she could have been a serial killer for all I knew. I kept my pack close to my legs, in case I chickened out and had to make a run for it.

The moon cast its light into the room through a slit

between the heavy chocolate-colored drapes. The fairness of her skin practically glowed. It was almost translucent.

"What's your name?" I managed to ask.

"Shawna. Yours?"

"Jodi."

"So, what, dear Jodi, brings you to New Orleans?"

My mouth felt like a piece of leather that had been left out in the sun too long. I took a big swig of wine, its oaky tannins stimulating my senses. When I swallowed, my throat was warm and tingly. "My friends and I wanted to come for Halloween. I've been here before, but never for Halloween."

She stared straight ahead. "Yes, Halloween in New Orleans is something to see." Finally, she turned to me and looked into my eyes.

That tethered feeling was back, and this time, I had the sense that she was reeling me in.

"Is that all you came for?" she added.

The question startled me. It was as if she knew that something kept calling me back to this city. She didn't move her eyes from mine for a very long time, didn't even blink. I swallowed another mouthful of wine, nearly choking.

Shawna's body was so still, I wondered if she was even breathing. It was as if she were a statue, carved of fine marble. The artist had painstakingly smoothed out her face, making the features almost flawless, save for a small scar near her left ear. Her lips, sculpted in such a way that they looked plush, were tinted crimson. Her cheeks were high and firm, and her jaw strong but soft, and her nose had a small bump carved into the bridge. Whoever her Pygmalion was, I'd have to thank him, because for my first woman, the Universe had sent me a really hot one.

When I realized I'd been staring at her lips, I forced myself to look up into her eyes. She was patiently waiting for an answer.

"No. No, it's not," I said.

As far as I knew up to that point, I'd come to New Orleans to see the parade, take haunted cemetery tours, and get shitfaced. The feeling of there being "something else" had been vague. Not until that moment was I sure that I'd had another purpose for being there. I knew I wanted to taste freedom, I just didn't know that it had been summoning me. My mind roiled with thoughts that made no sense, and my stomach tightened at the knowledge that I wanted to sleep with this woman.

No. I wanted more than that. I wanted to spend a long, luxurious night gliding my fingers across her skin, brushing my lips across her opalescent cheeks, dimpled chin, and places farther down. I wanted to see her naked in the moonlight and watch her saunter to the breakfast table in nothing but a T-shirt in the dusky rays of morning's first light.

And more. Way more.

In a few short minutes, something about Shawna had wrapped itself around my heart.

These thoughts, unbidden yet undeniable, had just circled my brain and come to a stop when she took the glass from my hand and set it on the table. Her eyes narrowed slightly. "You know, if you do this, you can't go back to how you were. This will change everything."

"I know."

I'd been thinking a lot about being with a woman, and I knew that if I did it, it would alter the way I lived, loved, and saw the world.

She gently pushed a wayward strand of my hair out of my eyes. "You're quite beautiful," she said softly. Her fingers brushed the side of my face, and sparks and heat shot down my thighs. She took my face in her hands and stared hard into my eyes, and it was almost physical, how her gaze spiked through my psyche. Her face seemed to waver, then disappear, until the only things I saw were her eyes, and even those blurred into a hard, black surface beneath which swam pinpricks of light.

When she pulled her hands away from my face, my vision came back into focus.

"You were called here," she said.

"What do you mean?"

"To the city. To me. You want this."

I nodded, and she was suddenly on me, straddling me and pushing me back onto the couch. I didn't resist. She ran her hands up my arms and slipped them into my hair; her nails scratched gently against my scalp. The tip of her tongue was like silk as it glided from the base of my throat and up to the tip of my chin. A hard shiver made me tilt my head back. Nothing in my life had ever felt so exquisite, or so beyond physical pleasure. I felt like I was melting beneath her touch, and it took all my willpower to not come right then and there.

Her kiss was just as I'd imagined it would be—soft but demanding. Everything about her—smell, taste, touch—infused every part of me. I would give her anything she wanted. I opened my mouth to receive her and might have swallowed her whole if she hadn't pulled away to trail hungry kisses across my face and down my neck.

"I want…I so want…" I said through ragged breaths.

"I know what you want," she growled, and in an instant, two fangs sprouted in her sumptuous mouth and she plunged them into my neck.

The next few moments befuddled me, as my body quivered with a jumble of sensations—aching, burning, pain, pleasure. Mostly pleasure. Lots of it. I wanted more, and I wanted it from Shawna.

Even after my head cleared, pleasure lingered through my stupor. What had just happened? Were those really fangs? *I feel so weird.*

She was off me by then, and I was still lying on her couch. The reality of what had just happened hit me. *Holy shit.* She's a vampire. A *vampire.* Carefully, afraid of what I might find, I touched my neck, and felt the spot where she'd bitten me. *Slightly swollen. Jesus.* What were the odds of being bitten by a vampire? All the things I had read about vampires raced through my head. Was it true that you had to be bitten three times to become one yourself?

The answer was no. I immediately knew that something had

changed. And then I passed out.

I must have been out longer than I'd thought, because when I dragged myself across the room and looked through the curtains, the watery-blue sky of dawn was just emerging. Shawna appeared next to me and pulled my hand away from the curtains. "Come, you need to rest," she said softly. She led me upstairs and placed me on a bed.

✧

During my brief periods of consciousness that day, Shawna talked to me, offering soothing words in dulcet tones that made me feel safe. I saw her slip a card into my bag, and she said, "I'll help you with the transition. If you need anything, call me."

At one point, I was lucid enough to realize that I needed to make a call to Cecily, who was probably out of her mind with worry. Shawna was dozing next to me on the bed, and she stirred when I clumsily pushed myself up onto my elbows.

"Mmf. Are you all right?" she asked sleepily.

Even under the circumstances, I couldn't help but notice how cute she was when just waking up. "I need to make a phone call."

"Oh. Here." She reached over to the nightstand on her side of the bed and pulled a phone receiver off its base. "Use my land line." She handed me the phone, then got up and left the room.

I pressed the "on" button, but then couldn't remember Cecily's number. I stared at the buttons for a minute as if they were completely foreign. Finally, the number came to me, and I dialed.

"Hello?"

"Cee, it's me."

"Oh, my God! Jodi, where the hell have you been? I've been worried sick. Where are you? Are you okay? Have you been kidnapped? I've been calling you. Do you need the police?"

"Jesus, Cee. Calm down. I'm fine." Except for the raging headache and the little fact that I'd been bitten by a vampire.

"What's going on?" she said with repressed hysteria.

How was I supposed to tell her that I'd been bitten by a vampire? *Well, you see, Cecily, it's like this. I became obsessed with this gorgeous woman, and just when I thought she was gonna fuck me, she bit me instead. Yeah, it turns out she's a vampire. Oh, and by the way, I'm a vampire now, too. Don't count me in for the trip to the Pharmacy Museum. Love you. Bye.*

"Hellooooo? Are you there?"

"Yeah, I'm here. Look, something's happened."

"Oh, God! I knew it! Some weirdo kidnapped you and has you prisoner in his kinky sex cave or something."

I sighed. Cecily exhausted me sometimes. "No, Cecily. It's nothing like that." I paused. "Remember when I left you and said that I was taking your advice?"

"Yeah."

"I saw this woman, and I managed to meet her."

"Really?" She sounded a little calmer.

"Yes. And she wasn't just any woman."

"Huh?"

"She's a—"

"A dominatrix? A postal carrier? What!"

I exhaled. "A vampire." I waited a bit for her to respond, but after a minute of absolute silence, I thought I'd lost the call. "Cee, are you there?"

"Is this a joke?"

"Um, no."

She didn't believe me. But then, why would she? Vampires weren't supposed to be real.

"That bastard must've slipped something screwy into my drink last night," Cecily mumbled, obviously more to herself than to me.

"No, Cee, you heard me right. And there's more." I exhaled again. "She bit me."

The silence on the line was deafening. It was as if she'd stopped breathing. I knew that what I'd just told her was a lot to take in, so I gave her time to process it. When it had sunk in, I hoped she would be understanding and compassionate.

"Are you out of your fucking mind? Listen, when I said you needed something big to shake things up, I didn't mean that. You took it too far, Jodi."

"I didn't ask for it to happen. It…well, it's a long story."

"Jesus Christ. Jodi, stop it. This is not funny."

"Well, it's not like I knew she was a vampire and asked her to bite me, you know."

"So, what are you planning on telling your mother?" She was being sarcastic.

What *would* my mother think? Not that she cared much about what I did anyway. I'd have to think about that later. There were way too many other things to process at the moment. Heaviness was invading my limbs again, and my eyelids were closing. "Listen, Cee, I have to go now. I'll call you later, okay?"

"Wait a second. What are you—" *Click.*

Darkness enveloped me again.

I woke fully that evening, feeling sick and weak.

Shawna immediately sat next to me on the bed and put her wrist to my mouth. She'd punctured herself, and her blood dotted her skin like a jewel.

I sucked greedily at the wound, warmth and strength coursing with her blood down my throat. When I was done, she sat up straight. "How do you feel?"

"Weird." I pushed myself up on the bed and swung my legs over the side. *Am I really a vampire? Really? Or is this just a really fucked-up dream?*

"You'll adjust. It won't be long. You seemed eager." She crossed her legs and smiled, baring shiny white teeth.

All I wanted was to have those legs wrapped around me.

Jesus. As much as I wanted her, the reality was, I was a vampire. "You misunderstood," I replied groggily. "I didn't want you to bite me. I wanted you to fuck me."

Shawna stared at me for a moment, with what might have been a touch of horror in her eyes. "Oh," she said. "I'm sorry."

Sorry. She was sorry? She acted as if she had accidentally given me a chocolate cupcake instead of a vanilla one. "Sorry? You do realize that you made me *die,* and turned me into *an undead creature,* destined to suck human blood for the rest of eternity, right?"

She shifted in the chair and gazed out the window. "I really thought that's what you wanted."

"What made you think I wanted to become a vampire?" I slapped the mattress for emphasis.

"Many people do. It's not unusual." She turned back to me, and, with an intense, puzzled look on her face, said, "Besides, I looked into your eyes, into your soul, and I thought I read you. I thought that you were called here, that this was your destiny."

Something struck me then. Her words reverberated through my head. *I thought that you were called here.* That feeling that I'd been experiencing for so long, that feeling of being called back to New Orleans—was this what it meant? Was this what I was supposed to do? Was this, as Shawna put it, my destiny?

My life would never be the same. After thinking about that for a second, I decided that it was a good thing, because that's what I had wanted—a new life. Realizing that suddenly made me feel whole, and healthy, and alive. So to speak.

Hmm. Things were looking up. "Does this mean that I can do anything I want?"

"Well, no, not *anything,*" she said, sounding bemused by the switch in the focus of my questioning.

"I can go anywhere I want now, right?"

"Well, you still need money, you know. I'll show you the kinds of things that you can do for money."

"Can I fly now? If I want to pop on over to Greece, can I turn into a bat and fly there?"

She stared at me. "What?"

"Just kidding." Her mouth opened, then shut again. "But

seriously, I can do a lot of different things now, right?"

"Look, don't get carried away. There's a lot that you need to learn."

Only slightly deflated by her lack of enthusiasm, I considered the turn of events. Then, another thought struck me—I now had more to offer her. Although I would probably never be the mysterious, sultry vampire that she was, I was now at least part of the same world, with some of the same abilities. There was so much that I wanted out of life, and Shawna was at the top of my list.

I decided to make the best of the situation and stretched languorously on the bed, propped myself up on one elbow, and waggled my eyebrows. I still had not gotten what I'd come for. "Well, seeing as how you've made a grievous error, don't you think you owe me something?"

One beautifully trimmed eyebrow went up. "Well, you *are* feeling better." With the grace of a leopard, she moved to the bed and lowered herself onto me. Our legs twined and heat quickly built between our thighs, a burning that I felt right through my pants. The intensity of heat, moisture, and friction were sensations beyond any I'd ever imagined. My body had been replaced with one made for nothing but sensory pleasure.

"Oh, God," I said with a moan. "This is definitely better than anything I've felt with guys."

Fire turned to ice on my skin as her lips pulled away and she pushed herself up. "Wait. Are you straight?"

I looked at her, startled. "I was. I mean, no. Not really—"

That's when it all went to shit.

"Oh, no. No way." She got up and stalked from the room.

I went after her, panicked. "Wait! What difference does it make?"

She came back into the room. Nearly colliding with me, she grabbed my bag and thrust it at me. "I don't fuck straight women. Here you go. Nice meeting you." She pulled me down the stairs.

"You're kidding, right?"

"No, I'm not."

She shoved me to the door, and as she was hurtling me through it, my eyes met hers and they locked for a split second. She seemed disquieted by this, like a person who'd just had all her secrets revealed. And I think they had been. At least a few.

The one secret I saw there more than anything else was the pain of betrayal, layers of it. The worst part was that she thought that I had betrayed her too.

What I also saw was that her eyes had once been green. Not like an emerald or jade, but like a peridot—emerald-like but with hints of yellow. They had been breathtakingly beautiful, like the first sign of spring after a long, barren winter, and I wished they were still like that. In their fractures were the scars of deception, and I wanted to take them away, or at least make up for whatever others had done to her.

I saw all this in the nanosecond it took for her to push me through the open door.

"Go," she said, and she slammed the door in my face.

What a bitch.

But even at that moment, I knew that I might be in love with her.

∽

One thing I'd always had in any relationship was pride—if someone wasn't interested, I didn't beg. When I met Shawna, my pride abandoned me.

Back in my room at the hotel, I called Cecily, who was out having a good time somewhere in the French Quarter. "Hi, it's me," I said.

"Jodi. What the hell? What are you doing?"

"I'm working things out."

"Working things out? You mean like deciding if you prefer your blood shaken and not stirred?"

"Can you be serious for just a minute?"

"I am being serious, Jodi. Jesus Christ. Why are you doing this? It's not funny anymore."

"I need to stay in New Orleans for a while, to figure this

thing out." There was no way I was going back to my old life. There was nothing there for me.

"Figure *what* out? Would you stop with this? You're really starting to scare me."

I was. I heard it in her voice. "Okay, I met someone."

"You told me that."

"And I think I might be in love."

"Excuse me?"

"I might be in love," I mumbled self-consciously, knowing how it must sound.

"With some nutty woman who told you she's a vampire? What the hell is wrong with you?"

"I know it sounds crazy, but I've never felt like this before in my entire life."

"I'm sure. What with being undead and all."

After the sarcasm, I thought I heard a little whimper. "Cee, you okay?"

"Oh, dear God. You've lost your mind." Cecily's voice was a little broken, and I knew she was holding back tears.

"Don't worry, Cee. I'm still me. I haven't changed. Except for the blood-sucking part. I'm still not sure about sunlight, crosses, and all of that stuff—but I'm still me. I swear."

Cecily sniffled. "Jesus. You really believe you're a vampire."

"Cee—"

"All right, I'll humor you. I stuck by you when you decided to try to start a punk band, and when you were going to run off with that naked trapeze troupe, and when you thought that becoming a Druid priestess was your calling. And I will stick by you as you pretend to be a *vampire*. Christ." This last she muttered in that way that I knew meant *Only you, Jodi*. "But now who the hell am I going to go to the beach with? Natalie? I can only tolerate her for so long."

Now she was humoring me, like she thought I'd smoked some kind of wacky weed. But one of the things this vampire stuff conferred on me, it seemed, was a sense of clarity. Everything suddenly made sense, for good or bad. "Life is short. You don't have to do anything you don't want to do.

Except work and pay taxes."

"Speaking of which," she said, "what about work? Since you're going to stay here and traipse around the world with Queen of the Undead."

I ignored the jibe. "I'll call them and tell them that I've been in an accident and need to stay home a few days, maybe longer. Right now, I just need to buy some time."

"I hope this makes you happy, Jodi."

"I love you, CeeCee," I said.

"I love you, too, you fucking idiot. When you're done with your hot and heavy affair—I am just kicking myself for telling you to get laid by a woman—I'll help you pick up the pieces and get back to normal."

She still didn't believe me. I couldn't blame her. "I'll call you soon. Bye." I clicked off, my heart heavy that I would some day no longer have her in my life.

✍

The card Shawna had given me had her contact information, and I held it in my hand like a lifeline. I spent the rest of the night trying to reach her.

I called her, texted, E-mailed. Nothing. She totally ignored me. I ran my tongue over my teeth. Where were my fangs? I thought about sucking Shawna's wrist and it creeped me out a little, but just a little. It actually wasn't as bad as I'd always imagined it would be.

But I didn't know what to do now. Could I go out in daylight? For how long? How was I supposed to feed? Damn. I texted her again.

You turned me into a vampire against my will. I'd think you'd at least have the decency to respond to me.

That must have hit a nerve. She texted me back: *Come over tomorrow night.*

About three minutes after sundown the next evening, I was at her door. The swiftness with which I now moved kind of freaked me out, but it was pretty awesome. She answered the door and, clearly, she'd just gotten up. She looked gorgeous with her hair tousled, standing there in a loose T-shirt. My eyes drifted down. *And not much else.* Her nipples were visible beneath the shirt, and I wanted to touch them so badly that I could feel my fingertips twitching with excitement.

She held the door open for me, but didn't meet my eyes as I slipped past her and walked into her living room. A table lamp covered with a red scarf gave the room an ethereal glow. I didn't know if it was meant to scare or comfort me.

Before I got a chance to say anything, she spoke. "Look, I'm sorry. I really am. I misunderstood. I don't change anyone who doesn't want it. Usually."

"It's okay," I said. "Actually, I like it. I've always wanted to be invincible." I smiled.

She rolled her eyes, then gave me a half-smile. Relief seemed to relax her features.

"So how do you feed without changing someone?" I asked as I sat on her sofa.

"There's a way." Her eyes roamed up and down my body, and my knees trembled. The need to touch her became so powerful that I had to grip the armrest and squeeze. My nails dug into the buttery leather.

She looked at the armrest in alarm. "Remember your strength."

I released the leather quickly. "Sorry."

"Look," she said after a moment, "I'll help you adjust. I'll be happy to give you living space here. I have plenty of room. It's the least I can do."

"Thanks." She'd relented a bit, I saw, and at least I'd be close to her.

I thought I recognized sadness in her eyes. "You'll have to get used to lying. I apologize for that. It's a downside of this life, but there's no other way. It's a dangerous world out there for us."

I suddenly felt nervous about trying to convince Cecily of the existence of vampires. That had probably been stupid.

"You have a lot to learn," she said quietly. "But I'll provide guidance." She smiled, a little contritely. "All right then, let's get started." She stood.

"Sorry?"

"You'll need to feed soon. Have you discovered your fang mechanism yet? Some find it on their own." She gestured at me to stand, and I did.

"Um." I ran my tongue over my teeth and thought about when she'd changed me, about how her skin felt against mine, and her lips, and then the sharp, sweet pain-pleasure mix when her fangs sank into my neck. "Ow." I'd pricked my tongue on my fangs. Wait. My fangs? I gingerly opened my mouth.

"Excellent," she said. "Do you understand how they work?"

"Nah sure," I said, keeping my mouth from closing. I felt them retract. Damn.

"Fear can do it. And heightened pleasure, as well. As you get more comfortable in this life, you'll be able to do it whenever you want. Developing control is important. Watch."

She approached until she was barely a foot from me. She parted her lips just enough so I could see her teeth. Within seconds, her fangs had descended.

I stared. Her lips framed them perfectly. I looked up into her eyes, and a wave of lust and need washed through my chest and swept down my thighs.

"Your turn," she said.

Again I stared at her lips, slightly parted still. The glinting of the tips of her fangs and the memory of her on top of me triggered something, and my own rookie fangs slid into place. I kept my tongue out of their way this time.

"Yes," she said, voice husky. "Like that. Now withdraw them."

"How?"

"Blank your mind."

I thought about space. Dark, empty. My fangs retracted.

"Very good. One more time."

"Um." I hesitated. She was so close. All I had to do was lean in and kiss her.

"You have exquisite hair," she said.

"I can't do the fang thing if you say things like that to me."

She smiled, and I almost passed out at the sight. Vampires really were the sexiest things on earth.

"You really are beautiful," she said.

"Are you trying to distract me? Is this part of learning control?"

"Maybe."

"Maybe what?"

Her smile faded, and she took a step back. "I'm sorry. It's been a very long time since I've…mentored anyone."

I wanted her to trust me. "I'm not a player." They were just words, but I felt they needed to be said.

"We'll see." She didn't say anything else.

I extended my arms and waited for her to come to me. In her own time. Her eyes hardened for a moment, then softened again, like clouds being released from a storm. Slowly, she approached me.

My arms didn't waver, and I kept them high and wide to let her know that I wouldn't change my mind. Finally, she put her hands around my waist and held me tightly.

Her arms felt so good around me, so strong. Her skin smelled faintly of vanilla and her hair of raspberries, and she didn't stop me from kissing her jaw. Working my way forward, I was intoxicated by the taste of her skin—unhumanly sweet and tart. I nibbled on her lower lip, and when she didn't pull away, I kissed her.

Her mouth opened, and her tongue traced my lips. My entire body trembled now, and I burned deep and low. Our mouths pressed together harder, and our bodies were joined so tightly, we seemed to meld together. We sat down and she was on me, straddling my thighs. Her fangs protruded and her pupils dilated. I hoped these were vampiric signs of excitement.

"Oh, yeah," I moaned. "This is what I want."

As if remembering that something was on fire, she bolted up onto her hands, her brows furrowed in either disappointment or anger. I couldn't tell which.

"Please." I begged. I wanted this so much—to be one with her, to be a part of her and everything she did.

"No." she said, and she dragged herself off the bed. Her ivory-white fangs retracted and her pupils returned to their normal size, revealing flecks of gold and silver in her irises.

With trembling hands, I grabbed her shirt and pulled her back onto me. "Please, I'm begging you. You won't regret it, I swear."

"Look, I've told you—I don't sleep with straight women." She yanked herself free of my grip.

Propping myself up on my elbows, I gave her my most rational look. "You've already made me a vampire, and now you're going to let your conscience stop you from fucking me?"

In the soft lighting from white beeswax candles, I saw her jaw set with determination. Shadows from the flickering flames played on her face, and I thought I saw regret pass over her features.

"Making you a vampire was nothing for me, but screwing straight women always leads to trouble."

My body ached for her, and the hunger I felt bordered on the obsessive. And it frightened me, just a little.

Shawna may have been right—well, half-right—about me being straight, but she had freed me, in more ways than one.

"Okay," I said, "It's true. Up until now, I've been with men, but I've known for a long time that I like women. I just didn't know what to do about it. But you—I've never wanted anyone so much in my life."

She rolled her eyes at me again, crossed her arms, and leaned against the fireplace, her weight making the picture frames on the mantle rattle. "That's what they all say...before they go running back to a man."

"No. I won't do that. I'm different."

"They say *that*, too."

I had been looking at her first as a beautiful woman and then as a vampire, and my obsession had fixated on those facets of Shawna. For the first time since I saw her on that balcony on Bourbon Street, I was seeing her as a human being. Well, sort of.

There were layers of emotion in her face, same as anyone else's. Behind the shiny obsidian eyes were pain, pride, joy, anger, ecstasy, and regret, each one flashing brightly before settling back into the darkness, and the façade of apathy came to the fore again.

She'd been hurt who-knew-how-many-times over the course of however-long. But I was not going to let the pattern of her past ruin my future.

"Look," I said, as I extended my hand. She didn't take it, so I rested my hands in my lap. "I'm sure that your experience with so-called straight women hasn't been the best. Hell, I've known women who just wanted to experiment, but went back to men. And I'm sure they left some broken hearts behind."

Her eyes hardened to flint. That just made me more determined.

"But believe me when I tell you that that's not what I'm about."

Her shoulders hunched against anticipated pain. "Why should I believe you? What makes you so special?"

She had a point. Why should she believe me? She didn't know me. She only knew what I told her. What could I do to prove that not only would I not break her heart, but that I was, in fact, in love with her?

"It's not even about getting into a relationship and getting my heart broken," Shawna continued. "I just met you. What makes you think I'm interested in some sort of relationship? As far as I was concerned, you were going to be a one-night stand."

Well, that was just rude. "If you only wanted to have a one-night stand, why didn't you just fuck me? Why'd you change me, too?"

"I was going to do both."

I huffed in frustration. "Wow. This is a new one for me," I muttered.

"Messing around with straight women—even just once—is asking for trouble," she continued. "Because, you see, boyfriends and husbands get threatened. They find out that their wife or girlfriend slept with a woman, and they get freaked out and beat their chests and go after the threat. A man might never admit it, but he's suddenly concerned that the other woman made his woman come so hard that she'd never be satisfied with his performance again."

"So what? You could rip them apart, couldn't you?"

"Of course I could. Without breaking a sweat."

"Then what's the problem?"

She pushed off the fireplace and put her hands on her hips combatively. "Who the hell wants to put up with *that* crap? I have enough shit to deal with without having to break the neck of some stupid asshole who thinks his dick is the most important thing in a relationship. I'm fucking tired of it."

"Okay. But here's the deal. I know this sounds crazy, but..."

"But what?"

"But..." I'd never said it to anyone. Never. Yet I was so sure that this was what love felt like. "I think I love you."

She stood motionless for a moment, again with that eerie stillness. So still that I could have been looking at a figure in Madame Tussaud's wax museum. Then, she blinked and went to the bar cart.

"Don't be ridiculous." The amber liquid that she poured from a decanter sparkled in the light of a nearby lamp. Probably bourbon.

"I thought vampires didn't drink. Or eat."

She turned around to face me. "We don't have to, but sometimes it's fun." She tilted the glass toward me.

"Why is it ridiculous?"

"Because you don't even know me."

"Haven't you ever heard of love at first sight?"

Her spine stiffened and she straightened. "No." She took a gulp of her drink, then poured some liquor into a second glass. Finally, she came and sat down next to me and placed the second glass on the coffee table. For a moment, she seemed far away. She held her glass against her cheek.

I put my hand on her knee. "I think you have."

She stared at my hand for a long moment, then closed her eyes. Abruptly, she stood up. "You have to go. Now."

My inexperience with both being in love and being with a woman—not to mention being a vampire—had clearly interfered with my judgment. I'd been stupid and too pushy. I'd moved too fast.

"Look, it's nothing personal," she said, as she pulled me up off the couch and once again shoved me toward the door. "I just can't do it." She closed the door behind me with a controlled *click*.

Abandoned on her front porch, desperation invaded every inch of my flesh. To make things worse, I instinctively knew I needed to feed, but I didn't know how. What was I supposed to do?

I'd been a vampire less than two days, but already my senses were heightened to a level that shocked and exhilarated me. From nearby came the strains of music, drums, and cheering. The Halloween parade was in full swing. I'd forgotten that it was Halloween. *How appropriate.*

Cymbals and tambourines filled the air with their sharp tinkling, and I followed the sounds. I fell in with the crowds jamming the streets. The big, bright, and wildly elaborate costumes were an explosion of color and detail, even the shades of black and gray on the horror costumes, and my new depth of vision allowed me to see every quill in every feathery headdress and set of angel wings. The haunted house floats were massive displays of architecture and decoration, worthy of any design magazine, and the demons, skeletons, and evil clowns were the stuff of nightmares.

Among the costumed devils, werewolves, ghouls, and vampires were real vampires. I felt them. I also smelled them— a sweet herbal smell accentuated by notes of damp earth. And I realized that vampires had always been among humans, and I had never known it.

It was all so spectacular. And in the depths of my soul, all of it—the wild abandon, the intensity with which these people lived, and their conceding the supremacy of otherworldly beings—impressed upon me the importance of winning Shawna's love. I needed her.

My hunger would have to wait. I made my way back to her house and rang the bell. She opened the door and just stared at me.

"Shawna, please, just give me a chance."

She didn't speak or move, so I gently pushed my way in. I kicked the door closed with my foot and pressed her up against the wall. She continued to look at me with defiance, but didn't stop me.

I knelt in front of her. Slowly, I lifted the hem of her shirt, unzipped the pants she'd put on, and pressed my lips against the black silk of her underwear. She closed her eyes and moaned. Against her will, I'm sure. My mouth pressed harder as her hand firmly held my head, pulling me harder against her. Even a vampire with a will of iron can't resist the invitation of someone's face in her crotch. I pulled back and looked up at her.

"I don't have a boyfriend," I whispered. "Or a husband. Or any man in my life."

She leaned back against the wall for support. I thought I saw a tear in her eye. Could vampires cry?

I got to my feet and drew her upstairs. There was no resistance as we collapsed onto the bed. I pulled off her shirt, then her pants, and I ran my hands up her thighs. "You are beyond beautiful."

She rolled me over onto my back and quickly undressed me. Her black hair brushed my skin as she kissed my breasts and stomach, and it was like being teased by angel wings. Like an artisan working on her craft, she carefully, reverently touched me, and showed me what my freedom could be.

❧

A light breeze came in from the window, and a coolness touched my damp cheeks. I was sated but euphoric, senses heightened, pleasure still echoing down my legs.

Her hair was unbelievably soft and smooth between my fingers as I lightly played with it. She peered up at me with what looked like surprise…and bemusement.

"What?" I asked.

Propping herself up on one elbow, she said, "I told myself that I'd never, ever sleep with a straight woman again." She smiled sardonically, and her brilliant eyes held a glint. "How did I let you talk me into this?"

"Because deep down, you wanted it too." She looked unsure, so I gave her an engaging grin. "Besides, I'm not so straight."

She cautiously snuggled up next to me.

For the first time since I'd met Shawna, I felt truly safe. "And because talk is cheap," I said. I guided her head down to rest on my breast. "I don't just talk. I do."

The rope around my chest loosened, and I breathed deeply.

~

ABOUT THE

AUTHORS

LOIS CLOAREC HART

Born and raised in British Columbia, Canada, Lois Cloarec Hart grew up as an avid reader but didn't begin writing until much later in life. Several years after joining the Canadian Armed Forces, she received a degree in Honours History from Royal Military College and on graduation switched occupations from air traffic control to military intelligence. Having married a CAF fighter pilot while in college, Lois went on to spend another five years as an Intelligence Officer before leaving the military to care for her husband, who was ill with chronic progressive Multiple Sclerosis and passed away in 2001. She began writing while caring for her husband in his final years and had her first book, *Coming Home*, published in 2001. It was through that initial publishing process that Lois met the woman she would marry in April 2007. She now commutes annually between her northern home in Calgary and her wife's southern home in Atlanta.

Lois is the author of four novels, *Coming Home, Broken Faith, Kicker's Journey, Walking the Labyrinth,* and a collection of short stories, *Assorted Flavours.* Her novel *Kicker's Journey* won the 2010 Independent Publisher Book Award bronze medal, 2010 Golden Crown Literary Awards, 2010 Rainbow Romance Writer's Award for Excellence, and 2009 Lesbian Fiction Readers Choice Award for historical fiction. *Broken Faith* (revised second edition) will be published in print and e-formats in winter 2013 and *Coming Home* (revised third edition) in spring 2014.

Visit her website: www.loiscloarechart.com
E-mail her at eljae1@shaw.ca

L.T. SMITH

L.T. is a late bloomer when it comes to writing and didn't begin until 2005 with her first novel *Hearts and Flowers Border* (first published in 2006).

She soon caught the bug and has written numerous tales, usually with a comical slant to reflect, as she calls it, "My warped view of the dramatic."

Although she loves to write, L.T. loves to read, too—being an English teacher seems to demand it. Most of her free time is spent with her furry little men—two fluffy balls of trouble who keep her active and her apologies flowing.

Follow her on Facebook:
https://www.facebook.com/LT-Smith
E-mail her at fingersmith@hotmail.co.uk

EMMA WEIMANN

Emma Weimann knew at an early age that she wanted to make a living as a writer. She knew exactly how and where she wanted to write the books that would pay for her house at the beach and the desk with a view of the ocean.

Even though she has had those dreams for over thirty years now, neither the house nor the desk exist. Not yet. But she's working on it, and by now she knows exactly which type of wood her desk should be made of.

So far, she has published two short stories and is looking forward to seeing her first novel, *Crossing Bridges*, published in 2014.

Visit her website: http://emmaweimann.wordpress.com/
E-Mail: emma.weimann@gmx.net

JOAN ARLING

Joan Arling is a little hard to localize: She lives on German bread, French wine, Irish beer, and Dutch tobacco.

When she can afford it, she also likes whiskies from the southern coast of Islay. She's been a truck driver, a teacher, a drug courier, a rock musician. Her favourite pastimes are mistreating her guitar and spoiling her best friend's three tabbies.

Oh yes, reading and writing, too.

So far, she has published two short stories and one novella.

You can contact her at: JoanArling@gmx.net

DIANE MARINA

Diane Marina lives in the Mid-Atlantic US with her partner of 18 years. She is the author of several short stories published in the US, as well as a full-length novel, *How Still My Love*, which was published as a third of a trilogy titled *Triple Delight*. She plans to expand on the original story and re-publish the novel in 2013.

When not writing, she spends her time reading, hiking, running, and traveling. When she's not traveling, she's dreaming of all of the places she'd like to visit.

Follow her on Facebook:
http://www.facebook.com/diane.marina.96
E-mail her at: diane.marina@ymail.com

ERZABET BISHOP

Erzabet Bishop has been crafting stories since she could pound keys on her parents' old typewriter. She has only just learned that it is a whole lot more fun writing naughty books. She is a contributing author to *Sweat*, *When the Clock Strikes Thirteen*, *Corset Magazine: Sex Around the World Issue*, *Smut by the Sea Volume 2*, *Hell Whore Volume 2*, *Slave Girls* (upcoming) *Anything She Wants*, *Dirty Little Numbers* (coming soon), *Kink-E magazine*, *Coming Together: Girl on Girl*, and several other erotic anthologies and online magazines. She is the author of the Erotic Pagans Series: *Samhain Shadows* (upcoming).

She lives in Texas with her husband and nine furry children and can often be found lurking in local bookstores. She loves to bake, make naughty crochet projects, and watch monster movies.

Visit her website: http://erzabetbishop.wordpress.com
Follow her on Facebook:
https://www.facebook.com/erzabetbishopauthor
E-mail her at: erzabetwrites@gmail.com

R.G. EMANUELLE

R.G. Emanuelle is a writer and editor living in New York City.

Her university degree in English and literature propelled her into publishing, where she spent 20 years as an editor, typesetter, and graphic designer. She is co-editor of *Skulls and Crossbones: Tales of Women Pirates*, and her short stories can be found in *Best Lesbian Erotica 2010*; *Lesbian Lust: Red Hot Erotica*; *Women in Uniform: Medics and Soldiers and Cops, Oh My!*; *Lesbian Cops: Erotic Investigations*; *Khimairal Ink*; *Read These Lips*, Volumes 4 and 5; and the online collection *Oysters & Chocolate*. When she was child, a neighbor called her a vampire because she only came out after dark, so it's fitting that her first novel, Twice Bitten, is about creatures of the night.

When she's not writing or editing, she can usually be found cooking or developing recipes, as she is also a culinary school graduate.

Blog: www.rgemanuelle.com
Twitter: @Rgemanuelle
Pinterest: http://www.pinterest.com/rgemanuelle
E-mail: rgemanuelle@gmail.com

OTHER BOOKS FROM

YLVA PUBLISHING

http://www.ylva-publishing.com

YAK
Lois Cloarec Hart

ISBN: 978-3-95533-114-6 (epub), 978-3-95533-113-9 (mobi)
Length: 17,635 words (novella)

Leni, a small-town, blue-collar lesbian, despairs of ever finding true love—or even just a Friday night date.

Pickings are slim, but romantic woes aside, she's happy living in the place she was born and raised.

Then Leni gets a new job as a nightshift cook at The Jester's Court, a bustling roadside truck stop, where she encounters an enigmatic colleague nicknamed Yak. Finding herself fascinated with the woman, Leni disregards all advice to the contrary and attempts to befriend her fellow chef. Yak proves to be a hard nut to crack, but what's harder still is deciphering why everyone lives in fear of her.

When events spiral out of control and Leni learns the dangerous truth, she must decide if winning Yak's heart is worth the price she might have to pay.

LANDSLIDE
Diane Marina

ISBN: 978-3-95533-090-3 (mobi); 978-3-95533-091-0 (epub)
Length: approx. 7,000 words

Love and trust don't always go hand in hand. Michelle and Rachel live happily together in the foothills of Colorado. Rachel has never had any reason to doubt Michelle's fidelity, but when she hears a broadcast about signs your lover might be cheating on you, she begins to question Michelle's long hours at the office and the mysterious phone calls she's been receiving.

Does Michelle truly love her, or has she found love in the arms of another? Rachel hopes that a romantic Valentine's Day trip to the cozy resort town of Aspen will answer her questions and lay her fears to rest. Or will she return home with a heart damaged by an emotional landslide?

RICH GIRL
Joan Arling

ISBN: 978-3-95533-116-0 (mobi), 978-3-95533-117-7 (epub)
Length: approx. 16,000 words (novella)

Once upon a time, there was a rich girl who got kicked out of her father's mansion because she couldn't care less about knights on white horses. Instead, she wants her happily ever after with another woman—with Dawn, a cashier at the local supermarket, to be more exact.

"Rich Girl" is a fairy tale without fairies, but with a villain, not one but two damsels in distress, and a helpful sprite. No princes, no dragons, but cash registers and guitars.

SECOND NATURE

(revised edition)

Jae

ISBN: 978-3-95533-030-9
Length: 496 pages (novel)

Novelist Jorie Price doesn't believe in the existence of shape-shifting creatures or true love. She leads a solitary life, and the paranormal romances she writes are pure fiction for her.

Griffin Westmore knows better—at least about one of these two things. She doesn't believe in love either, but she's one of the not-so-fictional shape-shifters. She's also a Saru, an elite soldier with the mission to protect the shape-shifters' secret existence at any cost.

When Jorie gets too close to the truth in her latest shape-shifter romance, Griffin is sent to investigate—and if necessary to destroy the manuscript before it's published and to kill the writer.

TRUE NATURE
Jae

ISBN: 978-3-95533-034-7
Length: 480 pages (novel)

When wolf-shifter Kelsey Yates discovers that fourteen-year-old shape-shifter Danny Harding is living with a human adoptive mother, she is sent on a secret mission to protect the pup and get him away from the human.

Successful CEO Rue Harding has no idea that the private teacher she hires for her deaf son isn't really there to teach him history and algebra—or that Danny and Kelsey are not what they seem to be.

But when Danny runs away from home and gets lost in New York City, Kelsey and Rue have to work together to find him before his first transformation sets in and reveals the shape-shifter's secret existence to the world.

A TREAT FOR HALLOWEEN TRICKSTERS
RJ Nolan

ISBN: 978-3-95533-124-5 (epub), 978-3-95533-123-8 (mobi)
Length: approx. 6,751 words (short story)

Halloween has always been Jess McKenna's favorite holiday. She jumps at the chance to guide a group of foster children through a community haunted house—never suspecting that her partner Kim will provide her with a trick and treat of her own.

COMING FROM

YLVA PUBLISHING

IN 2014

http://www.ylva-publishing.com

CROSSING BRIDGES
Emma Weimann

As a Guardian, Tallulah has devoted her life to protecting her hometown, Edinburgh, and its inhabitants, both living and dead, against ill-natured and dangerous supernatural beings.

When Erin, a human tourist, visits Edinburgh, she makes Tallulah more nervous than the poltergeist on Greyfriars Kirkyard—and not only because Erin seems to be the sidekick of a dark witch who has her own agenda.

While Tallulah works to thwart the dark witch's sinister plan for Edinburgh, she can't help wondering about the mysterious Erin. Is she friend or foe?

BANSHEE'S HONOR

(revised edition)

Shaylynn Rose

Warleader. This is what the people of Y'Dan used to call the proud warrior Azhani Rhu'len.

Banshee. Oath breaker. Murderer. These are words that slip off their tongues now.

Azhani Rhu'len, once one of the greatest of Y'Dan's warriors, is now just a common criminal, escaping the justice of the kingdom she swore to serve.

~~~

Kyrian Stardancer. Goddess' Own. A healer and priestess, she is inviolate until one day, when her world is turned upside down and tossed over the back of a horse—literally.

Torn from all she knows, Kyrian finds her fate now rests squarely on the shoulders of the oath breaker, Azhani Rhu'len.

When signs of ancient evil appear, Azhani and Kyrian must choose whether to ignore the warnings or stand and face the terrifying menace.

When the Clock Strikes Thirteen
© by Ylva Publishing

ISBN 978-3-95533-155-9

Also available as e-book.

Copyright © 2013 by Ylva Verlag, e.Kfr.

Published by Ylva Publishing, legal entity of Ylva Verlag, e.Kfr.

Ylva Verlag, e.Kfr.
Owner: Astrid Ohletz
Am Kirschgarten 2
65830 Kriftel
Germany

http://www.ylva-publishing.com

First Edition: October 2013

Credits
Edited by Day Petersen and Astrid Ohletz
Cover Design by Amanda Chron
Cover photo by © photonetworkde - Fotolia.com
Printlayout: Daniela Hüge